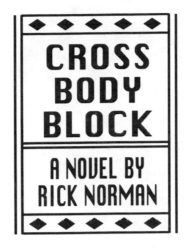

CROSS
BODY
BLOCK

A NOVEL BY
RICK NORMAN

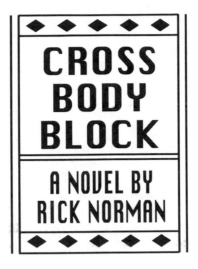

CROSS BODY BLOCK

A NOVEL BY RICK NORMAN

COLONIAL PRESS
BIRMINGHAM

Published by Colonial Press, Inc.
3325 Burning Tree Drive
Birmingham, Alabama 35226
1-800-264-7541

Printed in the United States of America
10 9 8 7 6 5 4 3 2 1

ISBN 1-56883-060-2

LIBRARY OF CONGRESS
Catalog Card No.
95-71611

Price $9.95

First Published 1996

Executive: Carl Murray
Project editor: Judith Faust
Cover design: Joyce Beatty, Athens, Alabama
Typography: Alex Nafe, Athens, Alabama
Reader: J. M. Cole
Typist: Ruth Manuel

COLONIAL PRESS   PUBLISHER   BIRMINGHAM

A hero is a man who does what he can.

Romain Rolland
(1866 - 1944)

For Tyler Riff Ferguson
(1986-1995)

and

Mark Kevin McCullough
(1951-1968)

Looking back with the advantage of twenty-five trips around the sun and about that many admissions to the V.A. hospital, 1969 was certainly the year to remember for a lot of people, including myself. The high point in my life came in November of that year when, in the short span of one week, I threw four touchdown passes in the state championship game and was guaranteed (under the table, of course) a brand-new, Mustang Cobra from Coach Bear Bryant for agreeing to continue my aerial assault for him at the University of Alabama. I was so preoccupied with trying to look, squint, slouch, limp, and mumble like Broadway Joe Namath that I barely noticed the tragedy that gutted Coach Fielder and his family that same week.

I recall being excited when the team selected me to deliver the eulogy, not because it was an opportunity to honor my fallen teammate or console the Fielder family, but because it would be my first chance to talk into a microphone, something I planned to do regularly as the country's premier college quarterback. If someone had told me that week that before I'd see another November I would lose six fingers and an eye in Vietnam or that I had taken my last snap from center, I would have laughed while I whipped his silly butt. We were immortal in 1969, funerals of teammates notwithstanding.

In reading this book, I sadly learned what happened to Coach Fielder and the remnants of the Fielder family and I finally realized what it was Coach Fielder was trying to pump into our swollen heads that championship season before we turned rabid and stopped listening all together: that "TAKE NO PRISONERS!" is not a motto to live your life by. Had I learned that lesson in November, 1969, I might be dictating this letter in a high-rise office rather than scratching it out left-handed and right-eyed in a double wide.

Mike Ross
Nathan Beford Forrest High School
Class of '70

1

It don't take long for your life to drip down your legs and into your socks. Four days ago I was being toted off a football field on my players' shoulders. One more victory and then the Promised Land. This afternoon my players were pall bearers, shouldering my boy. Looks like he beat me there.

I've come straight from the hospital, having myself just taken these stitches in the forehead from a fight with my oldest son. Now I have to go beg a judge I've never met before to set a lower bail so I can get another son out of jail before he dies or is killed, one. Not your average Tuesday, except maybe for Ben Cartright. I wonder if Ben spared the rod with those three boys of his. Most probably not.

I flew smack through the eye of World War II and seen things that still make me flinch twenty-five years later when they sneak up from behind and come shooting through my brain filter like a slug fired from the Texas Schoolbook Depository. But there's nothing in the universe worse than losing a child. Trust me on that. I've buried two now. A son this week and a little girl a few years back. And believe me when I tell you that if I don't get my wife's boy out of jail and bring him back home with me tonight, you might as well reserve a cell for her too. One with rubber walls.

If he'll listen to the whole story, I can convince the judge that my boy won't skip out on the court proceedings. He's not a criminal. He's only a teenager, and he's so torn up over his brother getting killed, it'll be hard to get him home with a shovel and a wheelbarrow. The Fielders, or what's left of them, ain't going anywhere. Can't. Wouldn't. We Fielders don't punt on third down. Which is not to say we don't punt plenty often.

We're all natives. I was born and raised in Smackover. I've lived here in Little Rock since college, 1950. Nineteen years already. Nineteen years. Time do fly when you ain't got a clue. Counting student coaching at Arkansas, I've coached high school ball of one kind or another an even twenty. For right now anyway, according to your twenty-five-cent official program, I'm the interim head football coach at Nathan Bedford Forrest High, the emphasis being on the *interim*. And we're on the final rung of the state playoff ladder. One game left for the whole nest of nuts. Maybe for the salvage rights to my life.

The Fielder family lives, and I use that term loosely, across town in a four-bedroom, two-bath-brick house surrounded by other four-bedroom, two-bath brick houses that are exactly the same as mine except for the color of the brick and the height of the lawn. Because I have, or had, a couple of able-bodied teenage boys old enough to cut my yard, my grass stays higher than everyone else's in my subdivision.

My wife and kids don't talk to me much any more as a rule unless they want something that costs money or unless I ask them an easy question *and* stand in their way so they can't pass until they answer. Every day I wonder how I got wherever it is I am. I can't tell what's receding faster, my hairline, my gumline, or the memory of my dreams. My future sure ain't what it used to be.

Except maybe for the fact that I pitched a few innings in the major leagues back before the Japs decided to cut my career short, I'm no different than ninety-nine percent of the other guys that got sent off to war. I came back slightly worse for wear as you can see, married the girl next door, and went to college on the G.I. Bill. Straight by the book. Then I started drafting a family, first adopting, then having kids and raising them the best I knew how. But not one of them came with an instruction manual that I ever saw. And no two were alike.

Somewhere I had got the crazy notion that if you just fed them, wormed them, kept their ears fairly clean, and loved them with all your might, somehow everything would turn out okay in the end. Well, this is as close to *the end* as I want to get, and it ain't "Ozzie and Harriet". Not from where I sit.

Turns out, in addition to everything else you have to do just to keep them alive until they're old enough to cuss you out and leave home, you have to teach them right from wrong. And that means trying to discipline them. That's the rub. Nobody ever tells you the right way to do it. All you know is what your parents did to you and that what they did was wrong.

You can discipline the easy way, on automatic pilot, and either pistol whip them regular whether they need it or not, or do nothing at all and hope they don't kill you some night in your sleep and smear misspelled cuss words on the walls using your liver as a marks-a-lot.

Anything else requires some gumption and a lot of upset stomachs. And the bottom line is that whatever you do is most probably wrong and no guarantee that some cold, November night you won't find yourself about to go beg somebody in their pajamas for mercy.

The road forked for me early on. Right or wrong, should or shouldn't, I decided when my first was little that I wouldn't whip my kids. Instead, I did other things to discipline them, like send them to their rooms where they have radios, record players, weights, comic books, and Playboy magazines hidden under their mattresses. Heck, I didn't have it that good on my honeymoon. Maybe I did spoil the child.

But you know, the earliest memory I have in my whole life is me and my two brothers clawing one another trying to squeeze into the little space above the back seat of my father's new Nash while his hairy arm whipped across the back seat striking at our bony legs like a crazed viper.

I had just started first grade when Pa bought a brand-new, black, 1929 twin ignition Nash "400". He loved it like the daughter he never had. More than life itself. Our lives, that is.

Every Sunday afternoon after church he would "give her a warm bath," he'd say, and lovingly sponge off a week's buildup of red Smackover dust, all the time singing some song he'd brought back from the Great War about what they were going to do to the farmer's daughters when they reached Paris. Then, in the best mood he'd be in until the next Sunday, he'd take the whole Fielder family for a one-car parade out in the country to some far off place where the people were bigger hicks than the average Smackoverite. And that wasn't no short ride. Let me tell you.

This Sunday afternoon that I'm telling you about, for some reason that puzzles me yet, I decided to immortalize my young self by writing my name in the red dust on the driver's door of his Nash using the toe of one of Ma's silk stockings. This was before Army scientists learned that red Smackover dust on a silk stocking will cut through the armor on a Sherman tank, given enough elbow grease.

Unfortunately for both me and Pa, I was just starting school and going through a stage where, although I had learned my ABC's pretty well, I was writing everything mirror backwards. When Pa hit his little lady with the warm hose water and realized that "Jackson Fielder" had been sanded down through the black paint and actually carved into the silver steel of his car door *backwards*, he went whoa-nelly nuts. He started yelling my full name at the top of his lungs. That was always a bad sign.

I remember being scared so bad the left side of my brain forgot how to walk at the same time the right side of my brain learned a new vocabulary word from my older brother Jugs. Kneeling on the throw rug in our bedroom, I told Jugs as fast as I could what I'd done and asked him to tell me quick what I should do to keep from being smote. He looked at me very calmly I thought, considering my father's voice was getting louder and closer even though my mother was trying to slow him down with some pretty good pass blocking, and considering my full name was now being mixed with cuss words also brought back from the Great War which were usually reserved for Germans and people who didn't pay their account at our furniture store. And my brother said that new word -- *flee*. Amazingly, although this was the first time I had ever heard the word, I instantly knew the complete Webster's definition and I followed his advice, bailing out of our bedroom window and fleeing as fast as my six-year-old, boneless legs would carry me. All the way to the top of the Smackover water tower.

The Smackover water tower was my Switzerland, my high-up, neutral place. On the walkway around the tank, I could sit all by my lonesome and watch my parents scouring the neighborhood for me while I planned their mutilation or, even better, the fatal accident for myself that would make them feel the worst for having lit into me all those times: with belts, with switches, with wooden spoons, and once, when I blew the car horn while my father was working under the hood, with a fan belt.

On my first mission over Japan, I remember looking down from a B-29 as our bombs ripped up the Japanese paper cities and thinking that something looked awful familiar. I had been there before. I was back up on the water tower, raining death and destruction down on the evil inhabitants. Sad to say, when you grow up, they actually give you the weapons to do all the things you dreamed about doing as a kid. And what's worse, you do them like you never learned no better.

When Jugs finally found me up on the water tower, tears rolling off my little nose and dropping a hundred feet, he swore to me that I had received full amnesty thanks to Ma and Jack Daniels, but that any further delay ran the risk of missing the window of opportunity, as I was holding up the Sunday drive to General Delivery, Dogpatch. We headed back down the ladder to earth two or three rungs at a time in a controlled free-fall so the window of opportunity wouldn't slam shut on my young behind.

That Sunday we drove for hours on corduroy roads in almost total silence except for the rattling of ice in my Pa's highball. All the windows were down and the red dust drifted through the back seat till our teeth ground like sandpaper. Ma, me, and my two brothers were minding our P's and Q's, or Q's and P's as I would have written them at that early stage of my education, and I was beginning to think I might actually live long enough to return for another week of first grade.

Well, Pa decided, since nothing had looked familiar for a couple of hours, he would stop at the next filling station. Not for directions mind you, that would be cheating. But so he wouldn't run out of gas trying to find a familiar landmark. And truth be told, he probably needed some more ice for his drink.

He hadn't even turned off the engine when the friendliest filling station attendant since Goober Pyle springs off a Gulf oil drum and comes running out to the car, looks for a second or two at Pa's car door, and asks Pa, "Filler up for you, Mr. Fielder?"

I'm sure the fellow was as much showing off that he could read as being friendly. He probably didn't even notice that the writing on the car door was backwards. It took Pa a full five seconds to figure out how this man at a one-pump station in the middle of darkest Arkansas come to know his name, but when it clicked, here come the tattooed cobra.

All of us boys caught some of it because there wasn't room but for one of us up next to the rear window. He batted us around the back seat like a triple-ball pinball machine. Lucky for us all, the tank eventually got filled and Pa realized he would have to stop swatting at us at least long enough to pull his wallet out of his back pocket and pay Goober for the gas.

As Goober stood waiting at Pa's window, Jugs saw another window of opportunity here, literally. He whispered his one word directive again -- "Flee!" -- and the next thing I saw was him bailing head first out the rear passenger-side window. I went to follow him but my little brother Jude, who also apparently instantly understood the word, had froze spread-eagle in the window and plugged it up like a paratrooper coming to his senses.

I gave my little brother a pretty good shoulder for a six-year-old, but all I succeeded in doing was making him shriek like a hamster in a beartrap. I might as well have sounded the alarm for a jail break. Never having lost a prisoner before, Pa reached around so fast for me he slung the money he was about to pay Goober into the back seat. With my little brother wedged in the back right window, I knew my only chance at escape would be through the window behind Pa. But that was on the other side of the backseat, at least fifty yards away. And now I would have to contend with the tattooed cobra.

Using my little brother's back to push off of, I plunged for the opening like a fullback for the goal line. My father's arm caught me around the waist at the one-yard line, just as I started my dive. As my head and shoulders emerged from the car, my father let out the loudest, vilest, longest string of cuss words ever to be hollered in Southern Arkansas since the last day of the Civil War. I'm sure they're echoing through the hills around that filling station yet, still knocking the chiggers out of the trees.

Lucky for me, the scream started Goober back-peddaling so that when I caught hold of his overall bib, he gave me the extra momentum I needed to break free of Pa's grasp. Which, it turns out, was only initially Pa's grasp. He had tried to turn me loose when he felt his right elbow passing behind his head but his Sunday cuff link had got caught in my Sunday belt buckle.

The three of us boys, joined now by Goober, hid out in the woods even after my mother got Pa to quit cussing. She finally coaxed us boys out by leaving three Nehis and the gas money in the gravel out behind the car. Goober never did show hisself before we left.

A couple of months later, when he finally got his arm out of the sling and could talk about what had happened without going for his belt again, he told my Uncle Woodley that in the car's side mirror he had actually seen the back of his right hand, still attached to my belt, come poking out the rear window.

If my father's blitzkrieg approach to discipline wasn't hard enough for us kids to fathom, my mother's was even more confusing. I couldn't have been much older than first grade when I rode one afternoon in the Nash with Ma to the grocer's. When we got home, she grabbed the two bags of groceries from between us off the front seat and, without so much as a look back, kicked her car door shut. My mother was like my wife, all business.

Well, instead of getting out on my side, I had slipped out behind her. It made me mad that she wasn't paying any more attention to me and that she could have just as soon slammed me in the door for all the care she took. My six-year-old feelings were hurt. So to teach her a lesson she wouldn't soon forget, I stuck my little knuckles in the door crack like my hand was mashed and let out a scream Johnny Weissmuller would have give his left coconut for.

Ma come up out of her pumps, spun around, dropped both bags on the driveway and drop-kicked a carton of eggs under the car with her bare foot. Along about that time I heard the first of several fingernails breaking as she scrambled for the door handle. I began to suspect she most probably was not going to laugh very hard at this, my first practical joke.

In an attempt to salvage the situation, I turned on my cutest Norman Rockwell, mischievous-kid smile, raised my little hand and wiggled my fingers at her, saying, "Ha, Ma, joke's on you." Before my lips closed around the "you," she had grabbed my little hand so hard all twenty-eight bones fused into one throbbing bulb. Then with her free hand, she swatted my head around the car not once but twice, with forehands and backhands Don Budge could have won Wimbledon with, all the time screaming, "I thought you were hurt! I thought you were hurt!"

How's that for mixed signals?

Now Coach Grote, on the other hand, I always envied him when it came to discipline. He's the fellow I replaced as head coach midway into this season. He'd been coaching high school football since they timed the game with a sundial. That is, except for the three years he spent as a Marine killing Japs in the Pacific. "There's no better training for coaching high school football than a world war," he was fond of saying. He was a master in the art of corporal punishment. He would tell me, "Fielder, don't be afraid to whip the kids regularly. Even if you don't know why, they do. And believe you me, they respect you for it."

He had a system, a graduated punishment scale, depending not so much on which of the Ten Commandments you broke, but on how it might affect the score of the next football game. It went: licks with your pants up, licks with your pants down, licks with your underwear down. It was a simple system, and justice, such as it was, was as swift and unbending as the business end of his customized cricket bat.

But I never felt there was much lasting wisdom being transferred through the end of that paddle. There is a fine line between teaching a kid right from wrong and teaching a kid violence. A kid's bottom just ain't a sensitive enough organ to be able to distinguish between a spanking, a whipping, and a beating.

Just like when you're grown nobody tells you the best way to discipline your kids, when you're a kid nobody tells you how best to survive the many benefits of discipline. When I was a kid, trying to figure out the best way to take one of Pa's lickings took up most of my efforts at concentrated thinking, especially in those few terrible moments after he would tell us we were getting a whipping but before leather actually began to fly.

I say "us" because I don't recall ever getting a whipping without my older brother, Jugs, getting one too. That was mainly because ninety percent of all the trouble I got into as a kid was from tagging along with him. But I ain't complaining, because ninety-nine percent of the fun I had was because of him. He was fun on a stick.

I admired everything he ever did, especially the way he took a whipping. He wouldn't cry. Not Jugs. He would more like growl way down in his gut like a lion or tiger till it was over. Then it would be my turn. And let me tell you I tried growling, howling, running in place, pretend dying, everything I could think of. But no matter what I done, I ended up crying same as my little brother and begging Pa to stop. No guts, no glory.

I remember once, Jugs and myself were on death row for dropping a dead possum down somebody's chimney. We were in our room listening to Pa slamming drawers while looking for just the right belt when Jugs tried to quickly pass on to me his survival technique. He told me the trick to not crying wasn't just the growling, it was also tightening your behind muscles so that your crack disappeared.

I had never noticed this part of his technique before because when Pa walked into our room to execute his sentence, he expected us to have already "assumed the position": pants around ankles, bent over the bottom bunk, two, four, or six buns side by side. If it weren't for being able to see Pa's shadow on the wall in front of us, we would have had no warning at all as to what was going on behind us.

Well, as much as I admired Jugs' growl, I wasn't real sure about my ability to master the muscular part of his technique. I didn't have too many muscles to start with, and those I did have below the waist were particularly famous for their frequent failures, especially in stressful situations. But this afternoon we were predicting a mild whipping by Pa's standards, four or five licks apiece, at most. Our crime was in the nature of malicious mischief rather than a violation of state law or one of the Ten Commandments. After all, we hadn't killed the possum.

We had found it fresh dead on the road. And it had not gotten stuck in the flue like the last cat had. Plus Pa was wore out from a hard day at the furniture store.

Our prediction was true. Jugs got only three half-hearted licks. When the shadow moved over me, I made a snap decision to give Jug's growling squeeze play a shot. The worst that could happen was that I'd start crying. At least that's what I thought.

Being many years older now, I think I can better recognize my body's warning signs. But when you're ten years old and scared to boot, sometimes your brain has trouble decoding all the impulses it's receiving. Looking back with hindsight, I think I might have concentrated too much on the growling at the expense of muscle control.

So when belt leather slapped my condensed bottom, I was as surprised as anyone to hear a high-pitched squeal coming from behind me, like the noise a balloon makes when you pinch off the blow-hole just right. I'm sure Pa didn't expect musical accompaniment either, and he held off a few seconds until the noise stopped. I saw his shadow disappear while he looked under my bed for the source of the noise.

The next swat brought the same squeal, but this time there was no mistaking where it was coming from. Knowing Pa and his knack for promotion, at that moment he was probably thinking "circus act!" I think he would have stopped altogether, except Jugs, probably with the same idea, says "Pa! It's whistling *Dixie*."

Well, this hit the wrong chord with Pa. I guess he figured we were being somehow disrespectful. So he started over on Jugs, then me, giving us a licking to remember.

The actual tune was a much debated topic around our house for years. But I can tell you from then on, I stuck to good old American crying.

My little brother Jude took a whipping different than Jugs or me. When Pa started belt hunting, Jude would curl up in a ball wherever he was, start sucking the thumb on his one hand and curling his hair with the index finger of the other. While Jugs and me were getting ours, he would look as calm as a frozen fish. But as soon as Pa told him it was his turn, he would shriek like a monkey on a high voltage line and keep shrieking until Pa stopped swinging, which was usually early.

Even though I never did like Jude, he made such a racket I was usually glad when it was just me and Jugs getting whipped.

Not that I would ever feel sorry for Jude, but I know now, looking back, that me and Jugs coped with those whippings a lot better than him. Jugs could get a whipping and then later that day run through a defensive back. I could stick a pitch in a batter's ear. But Jude, being an inside kid, couldn't pass the violence on like sports trained us to do.

Jude took to beating our dog. Jugs and me caught him one time, and Jugs snatched away the stick Jude was beating the dog with and broke it over Jude's head. It knocked him out for about five minutes. You know what? Pa gave us all three a whipping when he found out about it.

2

My wife and me never have seen eye to eye on how best to raise the kids. The funny thing is, here she is, the pretty, church-going lady and I'm the battle-scarred old coach. But she's the hawk and I'm the dove. After the war, back when we first got married, I used to think we were two peas in a pod. But we haven't been on the same farm much lately.

I made up my mind with my first son, Little Jackson, that I'd never hit him no matter what. He wasn't really my son; he was my wife's, and I adopted him when he was five. Her husband used to beat him black and blue. Well, I stopped that with a little corporal punishment of my own, and you can understand why I never laid a hand on him after I became his father.

You've heard of a love triangle. Well, we Fielders invented the love octagon. You need a program to follow my family, which is unusual for Arkansas, where oftentimes a family tree has no branches at all.

My wife, Dixie, grew up practically next door to us. She was the same age as me, a year younger than Jugs. That would make her two years older than Jude. She was a beautiful baby and kept improving from there. By the

time we were in high school, her father was patrolling the
yard with a blackjack to keep the boys from throwing
themselves against the windows like moths attracted to a
bright light. But being long-time neighbors, my brothers
and I were allowed into the compound pretty much at
will.

I suspect all of us brothers loved her early on, each in
his own way. Knowing everybody involved, though, I
would bet the farm that I loved Dixie earliest and most.
She, on the other hand, always loved Jugs. He played
football.

They got married just as Jugs left for the service. Dixie
was as happy as I was devastated. She had Little Jackson
while Jugs was off fighting in the Pacific. He was killed in
action before he ever got to see his son.

You know how low Dixie must have been, then, to go
and marry my snake-for-a-little-brother. I was myself
fighting in the Pacific and knew nothing about the
unhappy union until I came home and practically
proposed to her myself. I was crushed for a second time.

But I knew Jude, and I knew Dixie, and I knew they
would not live happily ever after. Sure enough, Jude
decided that beating kids was more sport than beating
dogs, and he figured since Jugs wasn't around no more to
stop him, he had a free hand. I caught him one night in the
act and convinced him that he should retire not only from
the sport but from the State of Arkansas. I must have been
pretty persuasive, because to this day he has still not
crossed the state line.

When he got to be a teenager, Little Jackson and I
talked one time about the whippings he got as a little boy.
It was at the hospital waiting for one of his little brothers

to be born. You'd think that if he remembered anything, a five-year-old who had been beaten by a grown man weighing one hundred and forty pounds would remember the pain. But he didn't or couldn't or wouldn't. He remembered only that he, his little self, must have done something wrong that caused his daddy to get mad and whip him. But he couldn't remember what. And still, when we talked about it ten years later, he was sure it was himself who was the bad one.

Those are the earliest memories Little Jackson has. Not too much different from mine, only more so. How's that for a foundation to build your life on? A foundation with red whelps and a crack down the middle. Maybe you can't undo it. Maybe once it's done, it's done. Maybe we've all been ruined in the name of discipline. Generation after generation, till death us do depart.

I'll never for the life of me understand why my wife Dixie didn't herself hesitate more to wield the rod. You would have thought that having watched her first-born son beaten by his devil of a father, she would have been the last person to lay a hand on any of her kids. But Dixie was the kind of person the world seems to be full of, who would rather have a set of rules to follow than to think for themselves. Because her folks had spanked her at the same time they were quoting from the Bible and telling her they loved her, and because she loved her folks, me trying to convince her that spanking our kids was wrong was like telling her that her folks were bad people or that the Bible might be mistaken.

Early on, Dixie and I had many a heated discussion about her methods of discipline. Every argument would end with her pulling her holy trump card and quoting from the Bible: "Withhold not correction from your child; even if you beat him with a rod, he won't die." The first time she told me that was in the Bible I called her a liar. I didn't believe it until she showed me line and verse. I heard it from her a thousand times since, and I still shake my head yet when I do.

She would explain to me that unless you could obey your own parents, there was no way you could be taught to obey God the Father and make it to heaven. Sometimes I had to walk out of the house, to flee, because I couldn't stand her dishing out King Solomon's discipline. Calling yourself a strict disciplinarian doesn't give you a license to whip kids. Maybe in the Good Book, but not in my book.

You probably are thinking how was it I practically killed Dixie's husband for whipping Little Jackson but wouldn't do a thing to save my own kids from the same fate. That's a fair question. I wish I could tell you. I've thought about it more than I care to think about. Maybe it was because Dixie spanked them rather than beat them. Or maybe she had better motives or something. But somehow, if I was five years old, I don't know that I'd notice much difference between getting beat by someone swearing at me and getting spanked by someone quoting the Bible at me.

But that ain't to say Dixie don't love her kids every bit as much as I do, in her own sacred way. And I don't mean to act like spanking is an everyday thing, or that when she spanks them she flies off the handle or draws blood. She doesn't do anything that isn't done every day in every house around the country. Heck, around the world. But my point has always been that just because it's done don't make it right or even okay.

To even begin to understand all what happened to us this week, you first need to understand about my wife. Courting Dixie was awkward for us both. My brother Jugs had been the love of her life, and his death had broken both our hearts. They named their son after me, for God's sake. My younger brother Jude had taken advantage of Dixie while she was still in shock and succeeded during their short marriage in doing the impossible: making things even worse for her. Me being the third Fielder brother, I'm sure she was praying for a Jugs, hoping I wasn't a Jude, and figuring something in between would be acceptable. Me, I loved her all my life and didn't want to be just *acceptable*. I wanted her to love me as much as I loved her; more than she loved Jugs.

For the longest time, whenever I would start talking about something that hinted at us getting married, she would make a little baseball joke about her being the Fielders' choice and then change the subject.

On my twenty-fourth birthday, I finally decided that since she was all I ever wanted, we were either going to get married or I was going to live with my mother the rest of my life and let Ma slowly drive me crazy. So I devised a diabolical plan. First, I traveled from Smackover to Shreveport and bought an engagement ring from an Air Corps buddy of mine. He always had a footlocker full of jewelry and a no-questions-asked return policy if your girl shot you down.

The next step was a proposing picnic at Rosie's Lake disguised as a birthday picnic. I got Ma to pack us a picnic lunch that Mahatma Ghandi couldn't resist. I also got her to take Little Jackson to El Dorado for the day. I packed my navy surplus one-man inflatable life raft which, if manned by two people, was guaranteed to ensure closeness.

My plan was to feed her, get her into the life raft with me, row her out into the middle of the deep lake, charm her, make her see that I was the Fielder she had been waiting for all her life, then pop the question. Since I didn't have a pocket in my swim trunks or my T-shirt, I cleverly taped the engagement ring to the inside of my thigh with some adhesive tape. If not for this last detail, I would not be married today.

Everything worked just right. The barbecue melted in our mouths and colored her lips a fiery orange. She gladly joined me in the raft, stripping down to her swimsuit so she could "catch a tan."

When we got in the middle of the lake, she shifted around so her back was to me. She asked me to put some lotion on her shoulders, which I did until my eyes rolled back in my head and I started to faint from ecstasy. Then she leaned back against me. It was as close to heaven as I'd been up to that point in my young life.

We drifted for I don't know how long, me trying to catch my breath and work up enough courage to pop the question. I noticed I was taking two breaths to her one. Finally, I came out with it, the speech I had been working on in my head for years: "Dixie," I said, "As best as I can remember, I've been in love with you since we were in the first grade. Even when I hated girls, I liked you. I know Jugs was the love of your life and Little Jackson takes up most of what's left of your heart now. But if you give me half a chance, you and me and Little Jackson could live happily ever after. Please, will you marry me?"

She said nothing.

We drifted along in silence, now three breaths to her one. Still she said nothing.

Finally, she made a smacking noise.

"Dixie!" I shouted.

"Oh! I'm sorry. I fell asleep. I ate too much. I feel like a fat snake on a hot rock." I got mad and almost blew the whole thing by not sticking to my speech. I blurted out, "Are you going to marry me or do you want me to live with Ma the rest of my life?"

She laughed and said, "Jackson Fielder, you're so silly. You don't want to marry me. You're just tired of living with your mother."

To prove I was serious, I reached for the ring on the inside of the my thigh. By this time, the heat had chemically bonded the tape with my skin. When I pulled, with the tape came the ring, the dermis, the epidermis, and a nice-size patch of leg hair. I started to scream but swallowed it down.

Dixie turned around, and I quickly palmed the tape which held the ring. If your fiancee is on the fence at all about whether to marry you, the first time she sees her engagement ring it's best it not be covered with curly black hairs. She looked into my eyes which were now full of tears from the pain and said, "Jackson! You're crying! You *are* serious."

I guess she didn't have the heart to turn down a crying veteran already related by marriage. The rest is history.

We got married in 1947, but only after the annulment of her second marriage and only after me converting temporarily to Catholicism.

One of the things Dixie and I always had in common

was baseball. She loved baseball as much as me even though she couldn't play a lick. She especially liked all the rules and statistics. As long as there are clearcut rules, Dixie doesn't have any trouble. But throw her in the briarpatch and she panics. She can't go to a grocery store without a list, or cook a dish without a recipe. She wouldn't try to hammer a nail without first going to the library and checking out an instruction book.

Dixie was the product, not of a broken home, but of a broken religious treaty. Her father had been raised Baptist but had converted to Catholicism so he could marry Mrs. Palmer. Coal oil and vinegar for sure. Somewhere along the way, he unconverted or disconverted and Dixie was caught in no man's land between the Old and New Testaments. After Rosie our daughter died, she got to relying on religion like kids on a nightlight. In recent years, she's taken to calling herself a "born-again" Catholic. Unfortunately though, I think her rosary got wrapped around her neck during birth and cut off the blood supply to her brain. And her heart.

Me, on the other hand, when they talk about hawks and doves, I was a dove back when we was just called chickens. I did my duty and went off to war, but it was by the hardest, let me tell you. I don't know that I was as much afraid as I was just plain sickened by all the violence and killing. Ever since I can remember, I have avoided conflicts and confrontations of all shapes and sizes. Except for a few spineful moments in my life, I've always followed the path of least resistance, and I guess that path has led me here tonight.

The first wrong turn I made on the path of least resistance lost me my oldest. Little Jackson is twenty-seven now and a professional ball player. A chip off the old block, some say. He plays for the Yankees, of all people. Maybe you follow ball. Maybe you've heard of him. He's a pitcher like I was once, back before tight pants and domed stadiums. That was way back before we went away to war and got taught that games are for kids. But he's done better than me. I didn't stick. He has stuck. I can't tell you how proud I am of Little Jackson and how much I wish he felt the same about me.

Before this week, when someone decided to flush the toilet that's my life, I hadn't spoken to Little Jackson but twice this whole year, once back in March when I called him on his birthday, and then last month after the Mets won the Series. That's months without talking to someone I taught how to tie his shoes and throw a curveball. I feel like I have to force myself on him to keep any kind of contact at all. He said he was glad to hear from me. He always says that. But if he was really glad, you'd think he'd call home every once in a while.

Anyway, I called him last month after the series, and I told him I had finally gotten a football head-coaching job. He said, "Great, Jaxdad. It's about time." I said, yes, it was. That pretty well used up *that* topic.

He said he'd had a good year and the Yankees had been in the thick of the pennant race, but that no matter what him or the Yankees did, '69 would forever be the year of the Mets. I said that was a shame and I wished they had done better. But between you and me, I have some real mixed emotions when it comes to the Yankees. If they only won the games Little Jackson pitched in and lost the other hundred and twenty or so, that would have been more than fine with me.

I asked him whether he could come spend some time with us in Little Rock now that his season was over. I said his mother missed him. He said he might. I told him his little brothers really missed him and wanted us to go fishing like we used to. He said he'd think about it. I told him I missed him, too. He said, "Cool," whatever that means this week. I hung up and one of the great mysteries of my life continued: What makes me the Bermuda Triangle of parents? Why do my kids grow up and disappear? Or die. What do I do wrong?

The impulse to flee ran deep through the Fielder family. Not long after Dixie and I first got married, Little Jackson took to running away from home. It was usually after Dixie had spanked him or threatened to, one. He would pack his little knapsack with his favorite toys, his swimsuit, and a snack or two, and would make a point of slamming the front door on his way to the schoolground down the street or to the house of one of the nicer neighbors. Me having been prone all my life my ownself to fleeing, I thought it was quite natural. Dixie, on the other hand, took it as a direct challenge to her and to God's authority, if there's any difference between the two.

The first few times Little Jackson ran away, Dixie would try her dead level best to ignore the fact that he was AWOL. That would work until she simmered up to a boil. Then she would go hunt him down, give him a spanking, and drag him back home by the ear. No matter how many times I saw it, it still made me sick in the heart.

I remember the first time I asked her could *I* go get him. She looked at me like I had lost my mind, me thinking I would be able to do better with her kid, her flesh and blood, than she could. Somehow, I convinced her to give me a try, and I started off down the street not knowing much other than there just had to be a better way.

It seems like it was just this morning, me finding him up in a tree at the schoolground. I tried to break the ice by asking what was in his backpack. He showed me he had his swimsuit in case someone happened to invite him to go for a swim, enough Fig Newtons to last me several lifetimes, and the spinning top I had given him for his birthday. I bought it not knowing that, at age five, he was too young to work it. But I was proud he valued it enough to pack it anyway.

Breaking the ice was a lot easier than talking him down and back home. We ate six pounds of Fig Newtons while I tried everything from promising expensive gifts to threatening to let his mother come get him. Nothing budged him, although after a half hour, the Fig Newtons started budging me pretty good. Finally, I told him he could go ahead and live at the schoolyard, but he should be careful to avoid the man-eating gorilla that lived on the school roof. He asked could he ride on my back on the way home.

Over the next year or so, until he decided home was probably safer and quit running off, I warned him about the thing with a flat head that lives under the manhole and grabs you by the shoestrings if you get too close, the half-man half-tree-frog that springs on you from above and sucks the juice out of you through the suction cups on its toes, and the Martian robot dogs, practically indistinguishable from regular neighborhood dogs, who were looking for small children and midgets to take back to Mars for their masters to kill, stuff, and mount on their walls. Just to name a few that come to mind.

This tactic didn't make it any easier to find him, because he would never hide in the same place twice, but it did get him back home without a whipping, which was good for us both.

Over the years I developed my own system of discipline-by-monster, using different monsters than the Bible uses and leaving out the rod. I'm not proud of my way or saying it was the best way, but I don't feel bad either, because it was the best I could think of with my limited mental resources, and it was definitely a less painful way than Dixie's.

Although I don't claim to have invented this system, I believe my innovation was relying on it exclusively to discipline my four kids. To the best of my knowledge, the technique was actually invented by my father as his alternative to whipping after he developed bursitis in the shoulder I wrenched out of the socket when I was in the first grade. He needed a replacement for the long, tattooed arm of the law.

For one example I remember, as soon as it started getting warm, us boys would get the irresistible urge to go swimming. That meant riding bikes to Rosie's Lake, which was nothing more than a glorified gravel pit that everyone around Smackover claimed was bottomless. It usually drowned a kid every two or three years. Their picture would appear the next spring in the front of the school yearbook with the caption: "Gone But Not Forgotten." Pa forbidding us to go to Rosie's Lake was like telling a pig to stay out of the mud.

One day, not too long after a retarded boy from Norphlet drowned there, Pa called a family meeting. He told us he had talked to the sheriff who had dragged the lake and found the dead boy, and that it turned out the boy hadn't drowned at all but had got into a nest of crystal snakes and was bit to death. I remember looking at my brothers wondering whether my mouth could possibly be as wide open as theirs.

Pa went on to tell us in a low whisper that crystal snakes were the most deadly vipers in the world, and before this boy got killed, the scientists had thought this species lived only in the sea caves off the coast of Austria. The sheriff suspected that they had escaped from some gypsies who sometimes use them to guard their wagons by tying them to the doorknobs.

Besides their poison that dissolved your vital organs to mush within minutes, these snakes were particularly dangerous because they were perfectly clear and could be seen only on the rare occasion when they were muddy or when they were "frenzying" on the surface. He described a "frenzy" as a solid, writhing ball of crystal snakes, half as big around as the water tower, all slithering in and out amongst one another, waiting for someone to swim by, retarded or not.

I remember asking Pa how could you tell whether one was around, if they were neither dirty nor frenzying. He said you generally couldn't until it was too late, but since crystal snakes are the coldest-blooded of all cold-blooded reptiles -- and here's where he leaned across the kitchen table and whispered -- you could sometimes tell a frenzy was near if you were to swim into a patch of unusually cool water, generally near the bottom. My brother Jugs swallowed hard and, after a few tries where nothing came out of his mouth, eventually admitted that he had felt just such cold spots during his past unsuccessful attempts to touch the bottom of the lake. I knew I had, too, but I was so scared I couldn't speak.

Pa got up from the table and rubbed each of our heads tenderly and as he walked away said, "I just thank God you boys don't go swimming at Rosie's Lake."

For the longest time after that family meeting, him telling us not to go to Rosie's Lake was like telling a pig to stay away from the slaughterhouse. But, eventually, the lure of the sea was too much for Jugs, and he decided, as he did repeatedly during his short but full life, to risk it all for a few moments of fun. I knew I couldn't talk him out of it, so I went along to offer whatever help I could.

Let me tell you, you've never had a headache like the headache you get on a sunny day from scanning the surface of a lake for transparent snakes. Jugs waded around for a while, then up to his waist, then up to his neck. I remember it as clear as yesterday, him saying, "I think Pa's pulling our leg. Come on in."

If it hadn't been so hot and if my head hadn't been about to rupture, I might have stayed up in the tree. But Jugs wasn't dead, or even bit, and I began to think maybe this was just another one of Pa's yarns. I waded in, an inch every ten minutes or so.

I had gotten up to my armpits when Jugs, who had swum out to the middle of the lake, yelled to me that he was going to try for the bottom. I screamed, "No!" but it was too late. He was under.

I remember counting, "Nine . . . ten . . . eleven . . . he ain't coming up . . . fourteen . . . he's dead . . . eighteen . . ." I stopped counting at thirty and started thinking about how I was going to break this to Ma. All at once the surface of the lake exploded and there was a gurgled scream the likes of which I've never heard. I hydroplaned back to shore and was halfway home before Jugs caught up with me.

When he did, he was laughing like Woody Woodpecker. I was crying hysterically. I started swinging at him before he finally got me calmed down. I was mad, mad as I've ever been. I thought I was mad at Jugs, but he convinced me I was really mad at Pa. Pa had started this crystal snake prank. Pa had created the monster.

Jugs told me he had a plan to get even with Pa and that the plan was so well thought out, Pa more than likely couldn't punish us for it. A double bonus. I said to count me in. Like there was ever a question.

We passed by the back of our store on the way home and Jugs picked out a cardboard box the size a lampshade would fit in. He cut a little square hole in one end about the size of your hand. Over the hole he glued a piece of screen. Over and under the screen he wrote with a crayola: "Danger! Crystal Snake. Poisonous!" He folded the box flaps shut on top and put a couple of strips of freezer tape across them. He cut another hole in the bottom of the box just big enough to stick his arm in. Then he stole one of Ma's silk stockings and painted a saber-toothed face on the toe. When I saw that snake face, a light went on. My brother never made a "B" in his life, much less an "A". But he was, in his own way, a genius. The Einstein of pure fun.

Jugs waited till Saturday, when he knew the furniture store would be as crowded as it would be all week. Then he called Pa on the phone and told him we had caught a giant crystal snake. Pa couldn't believe it. He said he wanted to see it. The trap was set.

Pa, everyone that worked for him, and six or seven customers were waiting for us when we walked into the store. I don't know who was grinning wider, us or them. Me and Jugs were both holding the box about chest high, acting like it was heavy, but trying to disguise the fact that Jugs had one arm dressed in Ma's stocking and poked through the bottom of the box. Nobody noticed.

Pa made a big deal out of the snake, announcing to the crowd that his boys had captured a dreaded crystal snake. I saw him wink at a couple of his salesmen. He read the front of our box with great fanfare. They all laughed. I heard one of the customer ladies say, "How cute." Pa had it figured that this was a juvenile joke. He wasn't quite sure what the punchline was, but he was playing along like grownups do, humoring their "young 'uns." Little did he know.

Jugs told him we had a six foot crystal snake in the box and that we had found it on the bank of Rosie's Lake, being able to see it because it was muddy. He told Pa to look for himself, pointing out the little screened window in the front of the box.

Pa glanced around the audience and, with a big smile, looked in the window. He said it was too dark to see anything. Jugs told him to look again. He got a little closer to the window, but still said he couldn't see anything.

About then, I could tell from a new wrinkle on Pa's face that he had caught a glimpse of movement inside the box. Jugs must have moved his arm a little, getting it in position. Pa quit smiling and asked in his business voice, "Do you boys really have a snake in there?" Jugs and me at the same time said the same thing: "Look!"

Pa got even closer to the window and squinted. His nose was almost touching the screen. He was really looking.

I was watching Pa's face and saw his eyes pop out just as Jugs punched his hand through the screen and pinched Pa's nose. Pa pulled away grabbing his nose and screamed out the worst of all cuss words at the top of his lungs. He fell backwards over a coffee table and cracked his elbow on the arm of a wooden chair.

Jugs slung the box off his arm, and we had the good sense to use our energy for running instead of laughing, at least until we got out in the street. Luckily, Pa had enough sense to use his energy for customer relations rather than chasing us.

After that episode, Pa experimented with other techniques for discipline. But, without his belt or his monsters, he never really regained control of his boys. I know the feeling. In the last week, I've had one son murdered, one put in jail, and one's show of affection landed me in the emergency room this afternoon. I've lost control of the horizontal, the vertical, and all points in between. The world feels like it's off its axle.

3

Over the years, my marriage has gone from puppy love to a dog's life. I will admit, though, that for the first six or seven years, there's never been a happier family than ours. Every night we got on our knees and thanked God that He spared my life in the war, let us marry and adopt her son. And that He gave us Rosie.

It was 1948 when Little Rosie came into and then took over our lives. She was surely the flower of my life. I promise you, there's never been a prettier or sweeter little girl since God started keeping records.

Dixie and I were both going to college at Arkansas and I had started student coaching. I couldn't wait to get practice over with and go home in the evenings to Dixie, Little Jackson and Rosie. We were happier than a TV family. When I got home, Rosie was my little shadow, following me everywhere. She was my snuggle-buddy.

No question Rosie was her father's daughter. She played more practical jokes on me than vice versa, and I consider myself a black belt. Frogs in my shoes, lizards in my medicine cabinet, peanut butter on the backside of my steering wheel. With her and me, April the first was bigger almost than Christmas.

I stayed home from school on Rosie's last April Fools' morning because she told me at the breakfast table that a man who said he was from the Baltimore Orioles had called for me on the phone the day before and said he would call back the next morning. She said he wanted to know if I could still pitch. I waited by the phone like an ugly girl on the day before the prom until Rosie finally told me I had been had. Again. You have to know someone's soul to really hoax them good. And she did. She really could have been a contender.

Her being so mischievous reminded me of my older brother, Jugs, and I loved her all the more for it. She filled the spot Jugs left when he got killed in the war. Almost.

It was hard for me to correct her when she stepped over the line, but there were times, like with all kids, that you just have to do something. Before we found out what was the matter with her, we were running her from one clinic to the next, every quack with a different answer, but every cure involving an injection of some sort. And Rosie hated those needles. I can close my eyes yet and hear that little yip and see those big brown eyes full of tears staring at me like she was asking, "I thought you loved me, Jaxdad. How could you let this happen?"

That's why to this day, with all the regrets I have in my life, number one is me using those shots to try and discipline my daughter. At home, to get her to do something or not to do something, I would tell her that if she didn't straighten up, I would take her to the doctor to get another of those "be-good" shots. I don't even want to think about it. I can't believe I could be so stupid.

About three days after her fifth birthday, not too long after Francis was born, the doctors told us she had cancer.

I wanted to eat dirt and die. I've never been much on religion since I was a kid and somebody read me the story about God killing the little babies in Egypt. But I don't think it would have mattered what I believed in. With this -- I lost every bit of faith I ever had. On the other hand, Dixie went to the extreme the other way. She started going to mass every day. For her, everything, I mean everything, revolved around the church and the Bible.

Rosie was sick for five years. For Dixie, it was a roller coaster ride. For me, it was a straight off-tackle plunge to hell. For the first time since the war, I began having nightmares about dying children. Terrible dreams. Dreams that ruin you even after you wake up and realize they're just dreams.

Knuck, her little brother, was closest to Rosie in every way: age-wise, friend-wise, even size-wise. You've never seen two kids in the same family get along as well as they did. Rosie lent Knuck some brains, and Knuck lent her some brawn. They were a perfect match.

After Rosie got sick, Knuck would go into her room every morning and stack her pillows against the headboard so she could sit up. He would squat on the foot of her bed, and she would read stories to him or they would put a board on the bed between them and work jigsaw puzzles for hours at a time. She had a way of making Knuck believe he had figured out where a piece fit. Knuck knew it was important that she eat and always made sure she had something to snack on. He would have taken her shots for her if he could.

They let us take Rosie home from the hospital there right towards the end. One night we heard her fall out of her bed. When I went to go see about her, she was lying on the hardwood floor, dead. I'll always wonder why she was trying to get out of bed, why she didn't call me to come pick her up like she usually did. I cried like a little baby. Dixie prayed the rosary and said to nobody in particular that we should consider her dying a wonderful thing because Rosie was now with God and because she would never suffer nor sin again. "No," I remember thinking, "that's been left to us."

The ambulance came that night and took Rosie away. The next morning, I woke the boys and told them their sister had died. They asked me where she was and I said at the funeral home where they were dressing her very nicely. I told them they would see her one last time at the wake and be able to say goodbye. Little Jackson and Francis cried. Knuck jumped off the sofa and ran into Rosie's room. I gave him a minute to be by himself and then peeked in. He was squatting on the foot of the bed, staring at the half-finished jigsaw puzzle.

At the wake, Dixie took Little Jackson and Francis up to the casket to pay their last respects. Knuck said he didn't want to go up there. To tell you the truth, I didn't either. But I've been haunted with nightmares of my father because I didn't see him dead, and I wouldn't wish that on my worst enemy. So, I talked Knuck into going up with me.

Rosie was a wisp of what she had been, but she still looked like an angel. Knuck stared at her for a long time. Then, like a cat, he jumped halfway into the casket. I grabbed his loafer as it flew by my head and it came off in my hand. He kissed her, then scooted back out. I slipped his shoe back on like nothing had happened, and we went back to our pew.

I never did see Dixie cry through all of it, including Rosie's funeral. I know she loved Rosie. Every bit as much as me. But like everything else, I guess, even her love has strict rules to it.

From then on, except for a few good moments, living with Dixie was like living with Mother Superior. She took to reading the Bible like she was cramming for finals. She was harder on the boys than Coach Grote was on the Japs. If they did something good, they got a pat on the head and a quote from the New Testament. If they did something bad, they got a swat and a quote from the Old Testament. They got paddled so much they thought they were canoes.

You know what they call a home without a mother don't you? An incubator. I've lived in an incubator now most of my adult life.

I guess the Bible gives her all the strength she needs. Maybe she has too much strength, like Knuck.

The third great mystery in my life, after my wife and my first son, was my second son, Knuck. He was born in 1951, nine years behind Little Jackson and three years behind Rosie. His name is really Joseph, but Little Jackson started calling him Knucklehead early on because that's what the Three Stooges called each other. Somehow, it fit him and stuck.

Knuck's a big, strong, tough boy, which is good for playing football but not for much else that I can see. We held him back in the third grade, hoping his mind would catch up with his body. That was an unfair contest. So this is his senior year, two years older but one grade in front of Francis.

Francis, on the other hand, our baby, never had a mean bone in his body. As a matter of fact until here lately,

I didn't think he had *any* bones in his body. Francis was the kind of kid other parents like to tell you they have. If somebody needed their erasers clapped, he stayed after school and clapped them. If somebody needed a prayer said, he went to early mass and prayed his little heart out. He was a TV kid with a shiny face and Ultra Brite smile. Knuck called him Saint Francis the Sissy, and I've got to admit that sometimes he was so nice I could have killed him. Sorry. Stupid choice of words.

If I hadn't seen Knuck and Francis sitting side by side at the same supper table year after year, I'd never have known they were in the same family. It was rare they had a word for each other, let alone a kind word. Their only bond was their mutual fear of their mother. When she was in a soul-saving mood, there was the devil to pay.

Not too long after Rosie died, we switched from our old church to Sacred Heart Cathedral. I guess Dixie figured her old church had failed her and maybe future prayers were more likely to be heard coming from a bigger forum. Better connections. Or maybe bad memories. I don't know.

I'll never forget the first time I walked into that cathedral. I don't know if you've been there, but if you have, you can't forget it. Painted on the big dome behind the altar is a sixty-foot high picture of Jesus Christ from the waist up. I don't know when exactly Jesus was supposed to look like he does in that picture, but I know he couldn't have looked no worse late Friday afternoon on the cross. His face is dripping blood from all kinds of big thorns sticking into and out of his forehead. His hands and chest have gaping, bleeding, festering puncture wounds. And, for some reason still unknown to me, his heart is on the outside of his chest. It's got a little halo around it, but you can still see that it's his heart. The worst thing about the whole picture is the way they drew his eyes: they follow you wherever you go in the church. There's no escape. I'm telling you, this thing makes a skull and crossbones look like a cherub. If I was God, I'd snap my fingers and give the artist who painted me like that a hunchback at the very least.

My younger boys, Knuck and Francis, they were only seven and five, and this picture scared them half to death. They sat all huddled up in the pew like field mice with a hawk circling overhead. Little Jackson was old enough that he thought it was "cool." Frankly, I sided with the younger boys. Whenever I was in church, I kept my eyes closed as much as I could. But I always had to balance my fear with the pretty good likelihood of dropping dead asleep.

Well, for a while, threats of a public spanking and excommunication kept the kids quietly sniffling during mass. But one Sunday, Francis got to crying so loud Dixie had to take him out of church. After that, for the next couple of Sundays anyway, it became a contest of wills as to whether the kids were going to stay in church and bother the faithful with their sniffling or whether they were going to get carted out by the nape of the neck and whipped in the vestibule. Knuck and Francis against Dixie and God. Who you think was going to win that one? The fix was definitely on.

Finally, Dixie got the keys to the church on an off day. I think this was before the Pope made her her own set. She decided, by God, her children were going to hold still for Jesus' love even if it scarred them for life in the process.

I can still see Dixie dragging them up to the bowl of holy water in the back of the church, blessing herself, and then grabbing the little boys both by the hair of the head and making them stare at the insides-out Jesus until they quit crying, which took a good five minutes. And then they only stopped when their little eyes ran out of tears. Me and Little Jackson just stood there in the back of the church looking down at our shoes and wondering whether it was us or Dixie or God who had things so crazy mixed up.

Going to the cathedral wasn't just an option at the Fielder house. By the time the boys were only a little older, Dixie had talked the Monsignor into letting them be altar boys even though the legal enlistment age was eleven. They served mass together right under Jesus' ten-foot-high nose two or three times a week for several years. I spent more time running them back and forth to church than I did sleeping.

I remember going to see them serve mass one Sunday. They did fine as best I could tell, ringing the bells at the right time and catching communion. No errors. What really amazed me was them talking Latin back and forth with the priest. I started thinking to myself that maybe this altar boy stuff wasn't just a waste of gasoline. How many kids that age do you know that can talk Latin?

When we got home, I asked them how they learned Latin so quickly. They admitted they hadn't learned the first word yet. I asked them what they were saying to the priest up at the altar, and they said they didn't know what the priest was saying but they were mumbling, "Hey batter, batter, come batter, batter, swing."

I don't know if them being altar boys made much of a difference as to whether they were better or worse kids. I could make a good argument for both sides. Even after they'd been altar boys for a couple of years, Dixie and I go to the mass one Sunday that they're serving at. I'm kneeling there with my eyes closed trying to remember who Old Diz has for me on the game of the week, and all of a sudden Dixie jumps up -- she's the only one standing in the whole church -- and clears her throat like she has a hair ball the size of a pom-pom. I open my eyes and look up at the altar and there are my two sons in their black and white nightshirts, locked in mortal combat, wrestling around on the altar, trying to poke each other's eyes out.

Everybody in the church froze for a second. Poor Dixie was trapped in the pew so she couldn't get to them to smite them instantly. The Monsignor was thinking pretty fast, I thought, and reached down and rang one of the little hand bells. The boys went back to their neutral pews and the mass continued.

I don't know how the audience scored the fight, but I thought we'd have to bury Dixie, she was so shamed. You can guess what happened to the boys when they got home from church. Dixie would start by saying to them what her father always said to her, "When you're on the wrong track, it's time to pull a switch." Then she'd make them go out in the backyard and pick their own branch.

When they did something Dixie considered especially sinful, in addition to the spanking, she'd make them kneel on her linoleum floor while they memorized a page of saints statistics out of the back of their missals. I'd walk by and they'd start crawling after me, begging, "Jaxdad, please! Jaxdad!" hoping I'd put them out of their misery somehow. I'd just shrug my shoulders and give them my "every pagan for himself" look.

Dixie would have given her right rosary knot to have any one of her three boys become a priest. Little Jackson and Knuck would have been long shots for ushers, much less men of the cloth. So she concentrated her considerable efforts on Francis. No more than a week would ever pass that Dixie didn't speak to Francis about his "vocation," as she called it. This seemed to be her favorite topic any time the whole family was in the car. The rest of the family, we would hate to drive past a church, because if Dixie hadn't said anything yet that day about the excitement of a career in the priesthood, crossing herself always seemed to set her off.

She'd tell Francis he should listen deep within his heart for his call to the priesthood, and he was sure to be getting one soon. But, then again, she'd explain that just because he didn't *actually* hear an *actual* voice didn't mean he wasn't *actually* being called. You had to have faith that even if you didn't hear the call, you got it. So it's the same as if you heard it. If you can figure that out, you're halfway to being a born-again, Bapto-Catholic.

I got fed up to here one time and told Dixie I didn't want any of my boys being a priest unless and until we came to the conclusion they couldn't do anything else worthwhile with their lives. Dixie said it was a good thing my parents hadn't felt that way or I would be a priest. It took me a good week before I took offense to what she had said. I just let it go. There's no use arguing with Dixie. She won't let you change her mind any more than she'll let you change the subject.

All Dixie's talk about Francis becoming a priest had

an effect on Knuck, too, because every time she started carrying on about Francis and the priesthood was another time she failed to mention that possibility for Knuck. He took it to heart. As he got older, Knuck became not so much a practicing Catholic as a practical Catholic. One night she asked him why he hadn't said his prayers. He said it was because he didn't need anything just then. It drove Dixie fanatical, and she stayed on him like a hen on a June bug.

On the other hand, I tried to keep the boys in line using my own discipline-by-monster technique. For example, as soon as my boys were old enough to wear shoes, they flat out refused to. Even years of my stories about thirty-foot long worms living in the intestines of little boys who were crazy enough to go barefooted didn't have much effect on them. They didn't believe me. That is, until the day they sure enough got sent home by the school nurse for worms. Knuck took it alright. He was a little older. But Saint Francis was mortified. He was always very neat and clean and the idea of real worms living in *his* bowels made him a little crazy.

It was really kind of funny. Hard as he tried, Francis couldn't sit still. He washed his feet until I was afraid his toenails were going to soak off. Knuck tried to make Francis freak out by telling him about giant worms nesting in his intestines and coming out at night to scavenge on the cookie crumbs among the sheets. But truth be told, Knuck was a little skittish his ownself until I promised them both that the medicine the doctor prescribed would kill the worms before morning.

After they were asleep and to make sure they remembered to forever more wear their shoes, I couldn't resist going out to my tackle box, getting some rubber worms and sprinkling them around between their sheets. Well, the next morning Knuck got up and never even noticed they were in his bed. But when Francis woke up, he started screaming like he had grown another leg in the night. Dixie was mad at me because she had to keep him home from school and put cold wash rags on his head until he quit shaking. I reckon my boys didn't have much of a chance with me and Dixie for their folks.

But I figured my way of discipline, strange as it was, was better than hers. And I stuck to my pledge not to whip them, although recently it's been by the hardest. The closest I came before this past weekend to abandoning my system and utilizing the rod was just a couple of months ago. I had watched them over the years get more and more sophisticated with their own practical jokes. The scare-the-passing-motorist joke was their favorite outdoor activity. They had started out years before by getting on either side of our street and stretching an imaginary wire across the road so the cars would slam on their brakes rather than risk breaking off their antennas. Then they found an old paint can top somewhere and would roll it behind cars and yell "hubcap!" hoping that the car would stop and the driver would get out to search for a missing hubcap that wasn't missing. They loved to make adults do something stupid. I was lucky, because for the most part they left me alone. I guess they learned early on I didn't need their help to do something stupid.

They worked on variations of the hubcap game, none of which was especially clever, until one day a couple of summers ago, they made a big advance. They invented Ray Bob. They took some old clothes, stuffed them with towels and rags, and made a fairly real-looking dummy. They never could come up with a decent head, so they would generally stick Ray Bob neck-first somewhere like down the rain culvert in front of our house and then pretend to be crying, hoping to get a motorist to stop and help the poor trapped kid. Or they'd find a parked car on the street and stick him under it with his legs out on the road like he'd been run over.

Folks got used to it, though. After awhile, most drivers tried politely to ignore them. Some of my players from the high school took to running over the dummy's legs just to make sure no one ever mistook them for civilized.

Over the course of that summer, everyone in five square miles knew our street as the one with the "dummy kids." And I became known as Ray Bob's father.

Eventually, Ray Bob was retired, after having caused probably less than a couple of dozen double-takes and maybe six to eight cars to stop. At least it kept them using their imagination rather than rotting in front of the TV. And it was good training for things to come. But I'm getting ahead of myself here.

Skip ahead a couple of years to this past August. While all the other teachers are still sleeping till noon, coaches are busting tail trying to get things ready for two-a-days football practice. Arkansas Quad-A war was fixing to break out in a few short weeks. The last thing on my mind at the end of the summer is what my kids are up to.

I'm coming back from a day of strategy meetings with Coach Grote, just having stopped off at the burger joint for supper, which for me is an extra large chocolate shake that

I stick between my legs every time I get a frostbite headache. It's about dusk, and I'm on automatic pilot doing about thirty-five through my own neighborhood, heading into the setting sun, when from out of nowhere comes a kid on a bike wearing a football helmet, and he rides right out in front of my car. Before I can even hit the brakes, I nail him. And him and his bike are bumping, scraping and crunching around up under my car. My one hope is that since he was wearing a helmet, there might be enough of his teeth left to identify him by his dental records. It scared me worse than I've ever been scared in my life. And I'm a veteran.

I stop the car, flop out onto the pavement, and crawl on my hands and knees behind the station wagon. This is at the same time some fat lady who's seen all this while watering her roses decides to flop herself on the ground and go into hysterical gyrations.

I'm kneeling down behind my car on my now bloody knees, studying what looks like a knight run through the blender, hoping I don't see any eyeballs or other recognizable organs, and trying to figure out how I'm going to get this kid's body untangled from his bike and out from under my car in time for his funeral.

My brain idled back so that it seemed like everything was happening in slow motion and under water. I remember trying to pick my car up off the poor boy and feeling for the first time the sharp, unmistakable pain of an exploding lumbar disc. It's a pain that has become all too familiar to me in the weeks since.

Around me, I could sense front doors slamming, people yelling, and the whole neighborhood slowly gathering in a lynch mob around me and my murderous

Rambler station wagon. But everything was muffled and fuzzy.

The first nonhysterical human sounds I actually understood were the yodelled words of a teenager whose voice was changing at that very moment: "Jesus, Knuck! Ray Bob scared the you-know-what out of your old man!"

As the neighbors wrestled with the hose-lady on the lawn and her screams grew fainter, I could make out sirens in the distance gradually getting louder. The pain in my back was traveling up my spine like a lighted fuse. I stood up and turned around slowly. My brain revved up again and hit the redline. For the first time, I felt the remnants of fourteen ounces of cold chocolate shake between my legs. I looked up from my brown crotch towards the direction of the teenage voice I'd heard, and my eyes met the four eyes of my two sons, surrounded by a pack of their wild cur friends.

Their wide eyes and wider mouths told the whole story. No words were spoken. But with the speed of light, my eyes sent them the unmistakable death ray message that this was the straw that broke the camel's back, not to mention my own; that this was finally the time my moral stand against whippings was to bow to the reality of primate adolescents. This was going to be the first day of the rest of their short lives.

Like my father and Zoro before him, I made a one-handed move for my belt buckle. The instant I shifted my weight from one foot to the other, they broke in opposite directions. But they would not escape. This time, I would take no prisoners.

I jumped back in my car onto another six ounces of

milkshake and stomped on the accelerator. My back tires burned rubber for three full seconds before the station wagon regurgitated Ray Bob and his bicycle bits from under my tailgate. The neighborhood men screamed in horror like women and the women spun and fainted into bushes.

One lady in a bathrobe and curlers, who had been watching the tragedy from half a block up the street, took the heroic action of stepping into the street in an attempt to stop me with a citizen's arrest. Watching *Andy Griffith* can be hazardous to your health, because for a split second, I thought about adding another notch to my front bumper by flicking my wrist and taking her out like I had Ray Bob. But instead, I waved at her with one chocolatey finger as I sped by at about sixty miles per hour. The second I passed her, I recognized her as one of the ladies that hangs out with my wife at church. She kicked at my car with a pair of furry slippers and screamed something I can't repeat. Let's just say it ain't in the King James version.

I combed the neighborhood for my boys for an hour, my belt wrapped tight around my chocolate fist. But my speed and my temper got reduced with the passage of time, as is predicted by Newton's fourth law. By the time they finally got up the courage or the hunger to come home, I had showered and was sitting in front of my bedroom mirror wondering how serious I had hurt my back and recalling some of the crazy things my brother Jugs and I had done as kids. They were my favorite memories. But without exception, every single favorite childhood memory I have ends with the mark of Zoro on my rear end.

I promised myself when I got up this morning that I would make it through the funeral without crying. And I would have, too, if during communion I hadn't noticed one of the priests wiping the back of his hand on his dress. I had watched my own boys serve enough masses that I knew what this meant. The altar boys were playing a game. A game invented and perfected by my boys there at that cathedral. It has no name and no rules other than "don't get caught". All you need to play is a priest, an altar boy, a shiny communion catcher, and a church full of unsuspecting parishioners.

The way communion is supposed to work is that as the parishioners present themselves to the priest for communion, they close their eyes, open their mouths and stick out their tongues. The priest throws in a tiddly-wafer and, generally, that is that. The altar boys are there with shiny gold plates to stick under the parishioners' chins just in case there is a misdeal. Which there seldom is.

The way this game works is the altar boys tap the parishioners on the adam's apple at just the right moment in an attempt to make them stick their tongue out a little farther and lick the priests' knuckles. It's like when the doctor hits your knee with his rubber hammer. You've got to hit the right spot at the right time.

These kids were good. Not as good as my boys, but good. The priests never suspected a thing.

I was the only person in the church who knew a game was in progress. My brother Jugs would have known, God rest his soul. Rosie would have, too. I don't know why I cried except that I felt like Iwas were the last of my species left.

Because of Ray Bob's last ride, my kids ended up

weeding flower beds and trimming bushes until their fingers were raw and mucking out the horse stable until they smelled like a septic tank frog. But football was cranking up, and with a new season, everyone's slate is wiped clean. No wins, no losses, no ties.

4

I don't think I've told you about our horse yet, but he's as much a part of this week as any of my boys. And he was as much a part of the family.

You haven't ever seen kids take to animals like those two younger boys of mine. They were like Noah, they had to have two of every kind that there is. And I got the job of Noah's stable hand.

Since they were old enough to watch *Roy Rogers*, they had been warting me for a herd of horses. Everything I knew about horses I learned from a Budweiser commercial. I didn't want any part of a horse because I once heard they lived for thirty years, and frankly, if somebody had told me that about my wife, I don't know whether I would have ever gotten married.

When Knuck was ten and Francis eight, they were putting a lot of horse pressure on me. Rosie had passed away not long before and there was a big void to fill. But I wasn't ready to try and fill it with a horse. I thought I might could sneak a couple of white mice by them as cheap substitutes. A pet's a pet, right? And it almost worked. The kids loved them. They were so cheap to keep that I even developed a soft spot for them, myself.

But Francis tied his mouse to a kite during a storm in some sort of religious ceremony. Evidently not tight enough, though, because the kite came back with an empty observation deck. We never saw his mouse again, although I noticed a fuzzy looking white spot that I couldn't quite make out on a neighbor's roof for several days.

Knuck, on the other hand, loved his mouse like it was a real, honest-to-God pet. He named it White Rose which, I'm sure, was his way of trying to fill a hole. It rode around in his pocket for what must have been a year. Well, White Rose eventually came up missing, too. Lost in the house. Knuck prayed so for that mouse to come back, I was afraid the boy was going to sprout wings and float up to heaven. Dixie took this to be a good sign.

Knuck set up a little novena or whatever you call it, a bunch of his mother's prayer candles, alongside of White Rose's tread-mill. And I'll be a silver monkey if six months later or so, we weren't eating breakfast one morning at the kitchen table, and out peaks White Rose from behind the refrigerator, looking fine except for missing three-quarters of her tail. I'm sure the little electric fan on the back of the refrigerator was what lightened her load, but I refused Knuck's request to move the refrigerator and find it so we could sew it back on.

Knuck finially lured the poor, scared rodent out from behind refrigerator with some marshmallows on a coat hanger, and when he finally caught hold of White Rose, he hugged that mouse up to his neck like King Kong hugged Fay Wray. To another Family, it would have been as touching a scene as the end of *Ol' Yeller*. Not to the Fielders. The ties that bind had stared to unravel.

Knuck made the well-intentioned mistake of immediately taking White Rose outside to let her play in the sunshine and fresh air amongst nature. But, as they say, nature is cruel. Dixie and Francis and I were standing at the sliding-glass door watching them frolic together on the picnic table when from out of nowhere the tom cat from next door swooped down, snatched up a squealing White Rose in his mouth, and disappeared through the back hedge before you could say "hors d'oeuvre."

Poor little Knuck flopped over backwards off the picnic bench and busted out crying like he was the one being ate. I thought we'd have to call Marlin Perkins to tranquilize him just to get him back in the house.

The strange thing about the whole event was that, for some unknown reason, me and Saint Francis, who had been watching this tragedy unfold, both busted out laughing at the same time and had to wait for about five minutes before we could go outside and act like we were looking for the tom cat. Dixie shook her head, ashamed of us both. But for a month we couldn't stop laughing every time we thought about it. Some kind of a poor excuse for a family we are.

The next day I got a phone call from my next-door neighbor, the one who fed the tom cat his main courses. He said his cat had left an offering of a dead white mouse at his back door and he thought it might be one of my boys' pets. I told Knuck about the call. He ignored me. In one day, he had written his pet off as if she'd never existed. It was scary. Since Rosie died, he has been growing a hard shell to protect his soft heart. Unfortunately, it wasn't the defensive shell of a turtle, but more the offensive armor of a German panzer.

After getting the call from my neighbor, I went next door, picked up White Rose and put her in a lunch bag for burial. On my way out to the backyard, I asked Knuck if he wanted to participate in the ceremony. Without even so much as looking up from the TV, he said he didn't. Francis grinned at me and said he wanted to. I had to hurry outside with the lunch bag for fear I'd start giggling again.

I let Francis help me dig a nice hole and he even said some words over the mouse in what turned out to be a nice ceremony as animal funerals go. I've been to worse, but I'll get to that story later.

I was about to drop the lunch bag into the hole when Francis asked could he look at White Rose one more time. I figured this would be something even a nine-year-old could handle. It wasn't as if there was a bunch of blood and guts. So I said, "Sure."

He opened the bag, stuck his face in it and then looked up at me with the look of sheer terror and screamed, "She ain't dead! You can't bury her. She ain't dead!" I laughed and reached for the bag, but he snatched it out of my reach and ran to the middle of the yard. He looked in it again, "She ain't dead, Jaxdad! Her eyes are open. She's alive!"

Now, I might not be an astro-physicist, but I have participated in quite a few rat killings in my day, and given enough time I can generally tell a dead rat from a live rat. And White Rose was no more alive than a rubber worm, open eyes or not.

I finally talked Francis into bringing me the bag and I reached in and tried to pull down the mouse's eyelids like you see them do to the dead gunfighters in the westerns. But it was no use. The garage doors were stuck. I pulled White Rose out of the bag to show Francis the obvious signs of death, such as the complete absence of guts in the body cavity. But only the eyes mattered to Francis. He pleaded with me not to bury White Rose alive. What do you do?

I was eventually able to bury the mouse, but only after filling the bag half full with marshmallows, poking it full of air holes and swearing to Francis that if White Rose *were* alive, and if she wanted to, she was an excellent digger and could dig out of the hole in a matter of minutes.

Knuck never even asked to see where White Rose was buried.

I felt so bad about laughing at poor White Rose and then botching her send off that I broke down and finally bought the boys a real horse. I figured getting a horse was a good idea for both my boys. Knuck didn't have enough love left in him. Maybe he could start loving a horse and work his way up the evolutionary ladder again to people. Francis had too much love in him, and I was hoping he could spend his extra on the horse.

I saw an ad in the Sunday paper talking about a "gentle, elderly horse, great with children." "Elderly" caught my eye. I was looking for a horse with three hooves in the grave. I didn't want to be slinging oats at seventy-six.

I snuck off to the stables by myself so that I didn't get anybody's hopes up. I saw once on *Gunsmoke* that you could tell whether a horse was any good by looking at his teeth. But it's one of those tests like kicking tires or thumping a watermelon: everybody knows how to conduct the test but nobody tells you how to interpret the data.

The fellow who owns the stables comes out to open the gate for me and before I can get a look in the horse's mouth, this fellow starts talking and I can't help but notice that he's got the worst set of teeth and teeth-bits I've ever seen. They're either black or yellow or gone, and no two pointing in the same direction. His gums looked and smelled like rancid hamburger meat. I was glad to get into the stables so I could smell the manure. It was that bad. He had a toothpick in his mouth but it had to be just for show. He pointed out a horse, and I looked in its mouth. I saw white. I was sold.

The boys were excited when I told them about it. They asked me to describe the horse. All I could be sure of was that it was a real horse. A real *old* horse granted, but still, officially, a horse. I told the boys the one condition I had was that I wasn't going to be the one to feed it for the rest of its life. Francis, at least, was excited and he swore to me over and over that he'd be responsible for him, especially being that he realized I'd probably be dead long before thirty years had run. Little did he know this horse had seen quite a few trips around the barn hisself. Of' course, I ended up feeding him every day for eight years, up until last Saturday night. But I didn't mind much.

Now, having a Bible-toting, scripture-quoting wife has very few advantages, believe me, but one is that she seldom gets the short end of any argument or business deal. I purposefully brought her to the stables to finalize the purchase of the horse. The smell of the stable owner's gums was as invigorating to Dixie as the smell of a leper colony to a saint. Him and her locked tusks and went round and round, first over the price of the horse, then over the cost of room and board.

I was starting to feel sorry for the old fellow when he made the mistake of offering to show Dixie his paperwork to prove how much it cost to feed a horse. Dixie whipped her Bible out of her purse, slammed it on his desk, and offered to show him the place where it says "Thou shalt not steal." That took the wind out of his sails. But he never really had much of a chance to begin with.

The boys named the horse Gale Sayers although he ran more like Y. A. Tittle. I thought Francis would end up marrying that horse, him and it spent so much time together. He spent so much time in the saddle, I'm surprised he could feel a whipping. Knuck rode it once or twice, then wouldn't give it the time of day.

I, myself, eventually became soulmates with Gale Sayers, although I only rode him once in eight years. The kids still talk about it. Knuck and Francis were in junior high and, from a distance, I had talked the old man who owned the stable into letting us have a team barbecue there at the end of the season. He said no until I threatened to send my wife around to see him.

Most of the kids at the party had never ridden a horse, and after they quit staring at the stable owner's mouth and pledging to brush regularly, I decided I'd demonstrate to them the fundamentals of horsemanship before I turned them loose in the pasture to see how many thirteen-year-olds you can load on an elderly horse before his legs snap.

The problem was that I hadn't been on a horse myself in thirty years, and if I ever knew the fundamentals of staying right-side-up on one, I had long since forgotten.

So, after a short delay acting like I was inspecting the horse for loose bolts or something, while really trying to figure out which foot to put in the stirrup, I swung up on Gale Sayers and rode slowly away from the boys, hoping it would all come back to me like they say riding a bike does.

I had walked the horse out a hundred yards or so when I finally figured out that you had to pull the reins the way you wanted him to go, opposite of the way you work an outboard motor. Having mastered steering, I turned old Gale Sayers around and decided I'd open him up on the way back. See what his old legs could do, so to speak. Show these city kids a little of the Wild West.

I dug my heels into the horse's ribs and let out a Rawhide yell, but before I could take another breath, the horse had run halfway out from under me and was galloping back towards the team party at about sixty miles an hour. I guess Gale Sayers figured if I could play Roy Rogers, he could play Trigger.

About three strides into the gallop, which to the non-equestrian is the equivalent of three hard kicks to the crotch, I had learned to yodel, come completely unattached from the saddle, and was in the painful process of sliding off the left side of the horse. That's when I noticed that Gale Sayers was heading straight toward fifteen cheering little rodeo fans and a fiery barbecue pit. The reins were still between my fingers but since both my hands were wrapped around the saddle horn for dear life, it didn't help much. My left foot was dragging on the ground and my right leg was sticking straight up like a periscope. My right knee was banging against my right ear with every stride. I started screaming for the kids to get out of the way, but they were yahooing too loud to hear me.

About twenty yards from the kids, Gale Sayers still hadn't broken stride, and my foot that had been on top of the saddle bounced off so now both my feet were dangling free. It was now just my white fingers around the saddle horn keeping me alive.

I couldn't see anything but the side of the horse, and I was just hoping that the kids had the good sense to know a trick rider from the village idiot and get out of the way. Well, that was asking way too much for a Fielder-coached team, but a miracle did happen. Five yards from the crowd of boys, for some reason I still can't figure, Gale Sayers stopped on a dime. That slung me spinning like a top into the waiting arms of my cheering little rodeo fans. The boys grabbing me kept me from sliding on my chin forty or fifty yards past the barbecue pit. They patted me on my back and complimented me on my impersonation of Hopalong Cassiday. I spit out horse hair for the rest of the afternoon.

For the longest time after that, I hated Gale Sayers. Well, not really hated him. Mostly I hated having to feed him. It aggravated me to teach all day, coach all afternoon, and then have to drive out to the stables and feed a horse before I could get supper myself. But how do you get rid of a horse? It's not like you can flush it down the toilet, or stuff it in a sack, put it in your trunk, take it out in the woods, and let it go.

It took a couple of years, but me and Gale Sayers finally reached an understanding. More than an understanding. A friendship. One of the boys, I forget which, on one of the few occasions when they fed the horse, had given him leftover pancakes and the old fellow got the colic. We called out the vet, and he gave him an industrial strength enema. Then he told me, in front of my boys, that *I* should walk him around because he would die if he laid down. I asked him how long I was supposed to do this, and he said until he gets well. I asked how this would reveal itself to me, a mere disinterested layman, and he said I'd know the horse would be okay when he finally lifted his head.

Well, I walked that horse around the stables all night in the cold rain, water dripping down the back of my neck. I fell asleep walking a couple of times. I decided ten or twenty times to get back in my car and let mother nature take her course. But I couldn't have faced going back to the boys with bad news or even no news. No, I was in for the duration.

About four in the morning, the rain started clearing. I started pointing out the moon and the different constellations to the horse, hoping he'd forget about his bellyache long enough to look up so I could go home.

Finally about sunup, he expelled enough methane gas to launch Sputnik, raised his head and so help me God, smiled a big horse-toothed smile. Just in time for me to shave, shower, and be at school for seven thirty to greet thirty-five pimply-faced civics students still puffy-eyed from ten hours sleep in a warm bed dreaming about having their own Mustang convertible and a clear complexion. From then on, I made sure he got only corn, hay, and an occasional Tootsie Roll. And he kept his bellyaches to himself.

In addition to reaching an unspoken understanding that night, we sort of became religious converts together.

The night of the great gaseous grin was the same night that I invented my own religion.

Like I said, my life hasn't hardly turned out like the way I planned. Heck, it isn't even a reasonable facsimile thereof. I had been a professional baseball player. I had made it through the fiery center of a world war with only minor injuries. I didn't want a free pass. I never expected to change the world, but I had figured there was more to life than struggling at work to convince fifteen-year-old boys of the benefits of voting and deodorant and struggling at home to keep my wife from ascending into heaven and taking my kids with her. And what's worse, I knew that even if I could stand to do this another twenty years, the most I could look forward to was retiring and feeding Gale Sayers in the morning rather than in the afternoon. I needed something to convince me I hadn't already been declared the loser by unanimous decision, that I hadn't already been mathematically eliminated from the pennant race.

I know religion works for a lot of folks. Look at all those poor Mexicans. They eat dirt four days a week but will crawl on their knees up a volcano if a priest tells them it'll help in the long run. Not me. I just can't buy it. I wish I could but I can't. Lord knows I've tried. How do I know *this* ain't the long run? Too much of it didn't make sense to me. Plus, I've got bad knees and now a bad back.

So that long night at the stables, with the lightning striking all around, the rain bombarding the corrugated tin roof, pulling that poor horse through the muck, somehow it came to me that if I was ever going to climb out of this crater, I was going to have to find a new way. Use some imagination. If nothing else, I've got imagination. But the point was, I was going to have to do it myself. Take hold of the reins of my *own* life so to speak. Why not invent my own religion, if that's what it took?

The first thing I did was to decide on the main-most man. I knew Christianity was named after Christ and Buddhism was named after Buddha. I wanted to find a hero a little more modern than sundials who, for my convenience, spoke English. No more Latin, thank you very much.

I went through the short list you'd expect: Washington, Lee, Roosevelt (Teddy not Franklin), DiMaggio (Joe not Dom). But one by one, I weeded them out for different reasons. A fifty-six game hitting streak is nothing to sneeze at, but I don't know if it qualifies you to head up a religion. Then again, I don't know if Mohammed could hit a curveball either. DiMaggio made it to the finals, but I figured him having married Marilyn Monroe might cause minds to wander during prayer. Statues of her might be hard to keep nailed down too.

Finally, it boiled down to between Lincoln and Einstein. Both had kind, well-worn faces. Both were wise enough. Both hated war and violence. Neither one combed his hair. I liked that for some reason. Don't ask me how I know, but I'm sure God doesn't comb his hair.

Einstein didn't wear socks. That was a big plus. Having blamed socks myself for my terminal case of athlete's foot, I could identify with him. Einstein was German and couldn't speak English very good. He lost points for that. But Lincoln had got murdered, and I wanted to have a less violent ending to my bible when I got around to writing it. I went with Einstein. Einsteinism. Me and Gale Sayers were thenceforth Einsteinics.

Over the next several weeks, mostly in the late afternoons at the stables, I went about formulating the Einsteinic bible. First up was deciding on how things were in the beginning. I had always liked the part in the Bible where God said, "Let there be light." Not particularly because it was in the Bible, but because that's what my older brother Jugs used to say when we were kids at the moment he lit his own methane in the closet.

By the way, my brother had a place of honor in Einsteinism. He was St. Jugs, the patron saint of the bellylaugh. God, I miss him so. Part of the Einsteinic baptism was that each convert receives a written guarantee that when you die you get back together with your brothers. Whether you were good or bad. No matter what. And you are kids again in your old neighborhood. And you get to sleep together in your old room. Forever and ever. Amen.

I decided I didn't want a long bible nor a lot of commandments. You get you a bible with a lot of extra stuff in it, and instead of people just helping people like the Bible plainly says, people spend all their time arguing over mess that God could care less about, like whether you can cut your hair on Mondays or eat a white goat with a bent spoon. You come up with ten commandments, and some people take that to mean that the other six million acts and perversions that human beings are capable of are okay.

My religion was going to be short and to the point. Streamlined. Aerodynamic. No priests. I hate anybody telling me what to do. No nuns. I hate people scaring me and my kids. No churches. If people are going to do something good one hour a week, I hate for them to waste that hour inside a church when they could be out helping somebody that needs help. No mass. I can tolerate the singing, but there are too many commercials in between. No commandments. That's too bossy. Just three rules. First, do as good as you can. Second, nobody hits nobody. Three, brush your teeth regular.

Over the months and years of feeding that horse, I worked out most of the details of Einsteinism. All in my head. To give you the *Reader's Digest* condensed version, God sees what a mess we've made of things and figures maybe He made it too tough because we ain't got a chance in the world of ever finding out what we're supposed to be doing with our lives. So He sends his nephew on his wife's side, Einstein, down to give us a clue. The clue is $E=mc^2$. Well, before you can say "slide rule," somebody uses the clue to build the atomic bomb and they drop it on a bunch of women and children in Japan. Boom!

God and Einstein say that's not exactly what they had in mind, but it's too late to take the clue back. Every kid from here to Timbuktu now knows about $E=mc^2$. But the key now is to figure out the good in it. I even started believing myself that maybe his formula was the answer to my life. If I could only figure out what $E=mc^2$ really meant.

I read every book in the school library on relativity and took to quizzing Mr. Bodin, the physics and chemistry teacher there at the high school. It didn't take me long to figure out Mr. Bodin might have been strong on Newton and he loved electricity like a sailor loves his rum, but relativity had not been a required course at his college. In exchange for him answering my questions on physics the best he could, he would ask me to turn the handle on the hand-cranked generator he kept in the back of his classroom while he held the leads. I would crank that handle as fast as I could with him yelling for me to go faster, his hands clenched around those wires until his knuckles turned white and his eyes rolled back in his head. Otherwise, he was an okay guy. But he sure loved electricity.

As you can probably tell from the fact that you ain't seen dashboard statues of Einstein around town, it hasn't exactly caught on. Not even among the other horses at the stables. Me and Gale Sayers were the only converts.

Like me, Knuck never rode Gale Sayers much in eight years. His last foolhardy ride is one reason I'm here tonight. But I'm getting ahead of myself again.

5

I don't know when it was I first noticed Knuck turning mean, but it wasn't long after White Rose got catnapped, as we used to call it. I never would allow a gun in the house, but that next Christmas I made the mistake of letting Knuck talk me into buying him a BB gun. I gave him a half-hour safety lecture and turned him loose. It was like giving a flame thrower to a pyromaniac.

After two hours, not only couldn't I find him, I also noticed I hadn't seen or heard a cat in a good while either. Within a couple of days, it became obvious there was a general decline in the population of neighborhood wildlife. I guess he was avenging the murder of White Rose.

I gave him one conservationist lecture after another, but once he got the smell of compressed air in his nostrils, the best I could ever really do was negotiate safe passage for pets other than cats and for some brightly colored birds.

It seemed like Knuck was always into something he shouldn't have been. Too much energy is what I'd tell myself. Boys will be boys. But it wasn't that simple. Sometimes I think he wanted me to whip him. That he was trying me. But even though I was tempted, I resisted, sometimes by the hardest. I thought if I could just get him some direction for his energy, he would turn out okay.

I didn't have any trouble getting him interested in lifting weights. He took to it like a puny inmate. He was never prouder than when he was about twelve and they picked him to be on that local TV show. You probably remember it, *Buster Sims, Future Champions*. For about ten years, it came on Saturdays at noon before the game of the week. That is, until Buster paralyzed himself jumping toupee-first out of some gal's second-story window.

The way the show worked was that Buster, girdle and all, pranced from one exercise station to another and had each different boy do a different exercise while he sold the TV audience miracle milk and memberships to his health club.

Well, on this particular Saturday, Knuck was supposed to demonstrate the proper way to do chin-ups. Everybody we knew within broadcast range of Little Rock was sitting by the TV watching for him. He was at the very last exercise station when the show ran out of time before they got to him. He had trained so hard he would have just died had it ended like that, but he had one more chance to show his technique because when they ran the credits, the camera would pan all the exercise stations and would end up on the last one, his chin-up bar.

As they gave the cue and commenced rolling the credits, all the boys, especially Knuck, started doing their exercises. But fifty seconds later, by the time the camera finally got to him, he'd already done about eighty chin-ups. He was bound and determined but the poor little fellow didn't have eighty-one in him. All us and the rest of Little Rock watched him hanging there, straining and twitching, eyeballs bulging, the little veins sticking out on his neck. He looked like a turtle with a hot foot trying to bail out of its shell. The camera was focused in on him for the longest ten seconds since Dempsey fought Tunney. He almost made eighty-one, bless his heart, but the show ended for good before the bar got past his eyes.

He was still crying when I picked him up from the studio. I think by then he was more mad than sad. The next day he yanked the swings off our old swing set and by the end of that summer had become a chin-up robot. By the time he was a sophomore, he was the strongest kid on the team. By the beginning of this year, his senior year, he was the strongest kid in town. And he had developed a violent streak usually associated with your larger carnivores.

Being a teacher, I encouraged my boys to watch as little TV as possible during the school year. But, being a coach, I did make an exception for the NFL and AFL games on Sunday afternoon. It used to be one of our favorite things to do together. Wholesome, family entertainment, right? I remember one Sunday Sam Huff, the middle linebacker for the Giants, squaring off after a goal line play with some offensive linemen. They shove each other a couple of times, then Huff takes off his helmet, signaling that matters are escalating. The lineman made the appropriate response by taking off his helmet. But this lineman made the mistake of dropping his on the ground. Huff bent down, picked up the lineman's helmet, and with a helmet in each hand, beat the crewcut off the poor guy. Francis was appalled. I must admit even I was a little bit shocked, and I'm a veteran. But Knuck loved it.

It stuck in his mind like your first freak show. I've seen him reenact that scene a hundred times since then, every time with a crazed smile on his face. I hope he never hears about that guy Lieutenant Calley.

Sometimes I think maybe it was me, his mother, Sam Huff and Buster Sims, all of us, had created a monster. Last year at a basketball game in somebody else's gym, Confederate Memorial High I think, the football players from both teams started trading insults across the court like they're prone to do when a game is close and they're separated by a hundred feet. School pride stuff.

I wasn't there for some reason, but Francis told me that towards the end of the game, Knuck picked out the biggest boy and started pointing to center court and mouthing, "Me and you. After the game. Me and you." As soon as the game was over, Knuck and this other kid go out to center court, and before the other kid can start the usual prefight ritual of finger pointing, chest puffing, letter-jacket shedding, and insults, Knuck catches him with a haymaker right in the mouth and two completely whole teeth skeeter across the floor like dice. Knuck was ready to rumble, but the sound of incisors rattling on the hardwood sobered up everyone else. There was dead silence in the gym for a couple of seconds until Knuck looked around at all the big eyes and green faces, smiled his Sam Huff smile and yelled out, "Home run!"

After that incident, I tried hard to pierce his shell with a heart-to-heart. But my heart never made contact with anything resembling a soft organ. I talked to Knuck for hours and still don't know whether he realized what he did was wrong. My homeowner's insurance company knew what he did was wrong. They paid the other kid's orthodontist bills and dropped me like a pyromaniac.

It didn't help soften his personality any that Knuck has as bad a case of acne as I've seen in twenty years of pimply-faced high schoolers. It's so bad, the skin doctors told us he shouldn't play football at all, with all the inevitable dirt and sweat and bruising. But what might have stopped another kid, Knuck used to promote his image as a tough guy. He talked our team trainer into taping his whole face every day before practice so it looked like a skull peering out from inside his helmet. All you could see was a pair of Chinese-looking eyes flashing around. It must have scared those sixteen-year-old quarterbacks who came up to the line of scrimmage, looked up and saw the grim reaper playing middle linebacker. It scared me, and I'm his father.

You'd never know the acne bothered him. He was too tough to let it show. But I knew. I was there in the locker room after practice when everyone else had gone home, to see him yanking the tape and bloody gauze off his face. At home I saw the way he'd look at himself in the bathroom mirror with disgust. I was there to see him cry on the way back from Oschner Hospital in New Orleans when the skin specialist told him there was nothing they could do for him until he quit growing, and then there wasn't much. I knew. A father might not know what to do about it, but he knows when his boy is hurting. Eventually. Too late sometimes.

But the biggest shock I ever got in all my years of parenting was the day I learned that Francis -- perfect Saint Francis -- was himself also deeply hurting. I had gone to the grocery store one afternoon with him and Dixie. Don't ask me why. Francis was probably twelve or thirteen, but he had been Mamma's little grocery helper since God could remember. Really, since Rosie died. He had a love for his mother usually associated with your pouched marsupials.

I was assigned the critical responsibility of pushing the cart. I had to stay within arm's length of Dixie and keep it between the cans. Francis was trouble shooting, picking up the odds and ends Dixie sent him for.

We had passed the produce aisle and were well into the canned goods when Dixie remembered she had forgotten to get a honeydew melon. She asked Francis to go back and pick out a good one and reminded him to make sure it was ripe by pressing the end of the melon with his finger and smelling it like she had taught him. He smiled the loving smile of a future homemaker and vanished around the end of the aisle.

I decided it would probably be depressing to watch him fondling melons with the blue-haired women, but couldn't resist. I deserted my station and hid out behind some bananas so he couldn't see me. I couldn't believe what I saw. He was grabbing the melons with two hands and jabbing his thumbs into them as deep as he could. Melon after melon. Violating every one.

He wasn't having fun. This wasn't mischief. This wasn't boys being boys. The veins on his neck were poking out worse than Knuck on the chin-up bar as he strained to punch his thumb through every rind. And he had a crazed look on his face that I hadn't seen since the war.

At first it scared me. It was so out of character for him, or at least to me it seemed out of character before that moment. Once I had seen it, though, a lot of things made sense. For all the violence Dixie's spankings had put into Knuck, I always thought they had done just the reverse and taken all the fight out of Francis. Until that moment, anyway. I was wrong. And how.

But standing there, I didn't know what I was supposed to do or say. My first reaction was to ignore it and sneak back to my cart. But something told me he needed serious help. At that moment in his life, he needed a TV daddy.

Francis was so worked up he didn't notice me until I put my hands on his shoulders. As soon as he saw me, he busted out crying. Within seconds, though, he had turned it off completely. Quick as it started, he was wiping the tears from the corners of his eyes and the froth from the corners of his mouth. I asked him what on earth was the matter, but he just stared down at the black and white checked linoleum and said, "Nothing."

I kept pressing, and after a couple of hard swallows, he said he was sorry and would pay for the melons but please not to tell his mother. I asked him why he would do such a thing, not in a mad way, I just was trying to figure things out. He said he didn't know. I asked him if he was mad at someone or something, and he said he wasn't. He admitted he had done wrong and deserved to be punished but again asked me please not to tell his mother. He wanted *I* should punish him instead.

It was time for a heart-to-heart. I knew for sure he had one. I took him out of the way behind the hanging bananas and said, "Listen, Francis, you're a good kid. A great kid. I've been fooling with kids for a living for twenty years and before that I was a kid myself and you're the best one I've come across yet. But I'm thinking maybe you might be *too* good for your own good. I know you want to do everything your mother tells you. You want to do everything *everybody* tells you. But there comes a time when you got to do for yourself, too. You've got something bottled up inside of you that, if you're not careful, is going to blow one day and kill somebody. Every time your mother tells you to do something, it's like shaking a hot bottle of Coke. The fiz is going to find a way out. Somehow. Someway. Someday. It's only a matter of time. Ignore it and chances are it's going to blow the top off the bottle and spew out all over the ceiling. But if you'll just barely lift the top a little bit at a time, it will come out slow with no damage done. You better start easing up on your top a little. Nobody ever said you had to be perfect."

Nobody, that is, except his mother.

I didn't know what else to say for a while, then I decided to give credit where credit is due. "I know I haven't been much help with your mother. I swear I've tried, but she pulls that Good Book out on me. And how am I supposed to argue with that? All I can say, Francis, is I'll try to do better if you'll try to do worse."

He smiled and I rubbed his head and we went back to find his mother with what we agreed to be a nice looking, ripe melon. Dixie had gone on ahead without us, and we caught up with her in the frozen stuff section pushing my cart. She pressed and sniffed our melon, let out a sigh of disgust and marched back to the produce aisle by herself to rectify our ineptitude. On their way to looking down at the floor, my eyes met Francis' for one tenth of a second as Dixie stormed off between us, and, in that instant, we both knew that it would never change. And I knew I would never be a TV daddy.

6

Having three brothers growing up and then having three sons, I was all the time trying to fit my boys into a familiar slot. Was Knuck more like Jugs, who I loved, or Jude, who I didn't? Could Francis shake off a lickin' like Jugs or was it going to turn him mean like Jude? But try as I might, it wasn't any use. They just wouldn't fit. It wasn't that easy.

No matter how I treated them or what I bought them, it seemed like all three boys would stop talking to me about the time they got to thirteen. It wasn't that I didn't try to talk to my boys, but I could just tell that, except for the fact I fed and sheltered them and gave them their allowance, I just wasn't as big a part of their lives anymore. My younger boys drifted away gradually. My oldest, Little Jackson, was all of a sudden. Like a stake through the pieces of my heart. I never had a clue what was coming.

School teachers, you probably have heard, don't get paid much. But if you give up most earthly pleasures and control your appetite, you can make it from month to month okay. I always gave the boys a modest allowance. Enough to go to a show and get a couple of burgers each week but not enough to get into trouble with. If they needed more for something special, all they had to do was ask. I might make them work for it, but they got to do all they needed to do, plus some.

As assistant coach, one of my many jobs is I have to keep up with the concession stand money. I collect the money. I count the money. Then I take it home with me in a lock box until I get a chance to go by the bank and deposit it into the athletic account. It's how we buy our baseballs and bats.

Little Jackson was a senior, two or three months away from graduation. He had already signed to go to pitch at Arkansas and had the world by the tail for all I could tell. He never asked me for extra money that I turned him down. That's why when the concession stand money started coming up short, I didn't suspect him until there wasn't any other suspects.

At first, I thought I had maybe counted wrong, but after every game, I kept coming up twenty dollars or so short. Nobody fooled with the money but me, and most of the time the lock box was within reach, so it wasn't hard to narrow it down to Little Jackson, no matter how hard I tried not to.

I asked him indirectly about it and he tried to change the subject. I asked him directly about it and he got indignant. He made me feel like a hunchback with warts for even mentioning it. Dixie made me feel worse than that. The very idea of me accusing one of the boys she'd raised with the direct help of God.

So I decided to set a trap like I had seen them do on Dragnet. After the next game, I wrote down the serial numbers of all the bills in the lock box and also marked them on the edge with a spot of Dixie's nail polish. I left the lock box on my chest-of-drawers, as usual, and went to bed. The next morning, I counted the money. Twenty dollars short again. As soon as I heard Little Jackson close the door to the bathroom, I went into his room. I found the marked bills in his fat wallet which had over a hundred dollars in it.

I felt like crying. I sat down on the floor of his room. I couldn't understand it. Maybe it was just a phase, I thought. And maybe Richard Speck was just having a bad day.

When he came back to his room, I was sitting there holding his wallet in the palm of my hand, like you would a dead mouse. Before I could say the first word to him, he lit into me with a string of cusswords that would have made Coach Grote blush. He accused me of violating his civil rights, framing him, spitting on the Constitution, wanting him to leave home, not wanting him to go to college, not wanting him to play in the majors, being jealous of him, none of which was in the least bit true. I just wanted him to do as good as he could.

Dixie came in on the tail end of his tirade and was about to jump in on his side when he stormed out of the house. She looked at me and asked me, "What did you do to my son?" I walked out too.

Little Jackson had fled for good. He never has come back to live at our house. Dixie got some of her friends from the church to keep him until school let out. Then he left for summer school in Fayetteville. His coach got him on a summer team there. I didn't get to coach him his last American Legion season, something I had been looking forward to since the first time I threw the ball with him.

Rosie had died earlier that same year and I was still numb. I thought nothing could hurt me at that point in my life. But Little Jackson fleeing killed me. Especially never being able to figure it out. That was the worst part. Never knowing how come. Wondering if because he was adopted, we just didn't have the right hormones or chromosomes or whatever to be father and son. Did those beatings by his uncle-daddy Jude make him so he would hate any father? If Jugs had lived to raise him, would he have turned out different? Of all my boys, he was the one who had been closest to me. Closest to being my friend. He was a baseballer. No doubt.

We never talked about the missing money in my family again. Nobody mentioned it. For a good while there, nobody said much about Little Jackson either. My little boys never asked me why Little Jackson wasn't living with us anymore, so I guess Dixie told them something. God only knows what, I'm sure.

What killed me almost as much as losing touch with them was that my two younger boys, the ones me and Dixie had, didn't go any further than they did in baseball. And here's Little Jackson, my adopted son with none of my blood, who's pitching regular for the New York Yankees. So much for hormones or chromosomes.

I, myself, am a baseballer too. Always have been. I like the fact that there is no physical contact, no time clock, no equipment to put on, no loud whistles, no straining. I also like the idea that even though it's a team sport, really only one player on a team is doing anything at any one time. Plus, you don't have to think too fast, especially when you're pitching. Somebody, someday might invent a better game, but they haven't so far.

On the other hand, my older brother Jugs was a definite footballer. Not that he wasn't just as good in baseball and basketball and track, because he was. But he loved cracking heads with people. He had a natural love for physical contact usually associated with your larger horned animals. Not that he was mean: he just found high-speed human contact great fun.

I'll never forget the afternoon I knew for certain I was a baseballer and my brother was a footballer, and I never the train would meet. He was in the eleventh grade, which put me in the tenth. This afternoon, we were at football practice and he broke into the open field with the ball. Instead of trying to avoid the safety, he decided he'd just run through the poor kid. He stuck his leather helmet right in the kid's face and didn't even slow down. The kid exploded like a snowman on a train track. This was way before plastic helmets with facemasks, and the kid was out cold. As the coaches tried to revive him, Jugs came back to the huddle, sorry he hurt the kid but not overly concerned. He had not done it in a mean-spirited way, that was just the way the game was played in 1939.

I noticed on the top of Jug's old foldable leather helmet, there right above his forehead, were four teeth imbedded in the leather, red roots flapping in the breeze. I almost lost lunch. As the kids say now, I was grossed out.

When I wouldn't stop pointing at the top of his head, Jugs finally took off his helmet and, looking at the safety's teeth, said, "Geez, that's terrible." Then he said to the huddle, "Look, with the way the teeth cast shadows on my helmet, don't it look sort of like that place in England -- Stonehenge." He was right. It did.

He left the teeth in his helmet for the rest of practice like a pearly hood ornament. *That's* the difference between a footballer and a baseballer. It's something decided at birth, like whether you're going to be lefthanded or have freckles.

Although they never met, Knuck was like his Uncle Jugs, a footballer all the way. Knuck just plain had too many muscles to play baseball. In baseball, his strength worked against him, and he refused to use what little intelligence he had to compensate. He was stubborn as a two-dollar mule. No matter what I told him, he always used the biggest bat he could find and swung it as hard as he could trying to pop the ball. The few times a season he was able to make contact, he'd knock down an infielder or, if the ball hit just right on his bat, he'd put one up against the fence. But killed infielders and dents in the fence ain't officially kept statistics, so it was hard to justify playing him.

I tried to make a catcher out of him because he was built like a rock, but, unfortunately, his hands were made out of the same stuff. He told me once he didn't much like the game of baseball because there wasn't enough contact. He said it would be much more fun if *everyone* wore catcher's equipment and *everyone* carried a bat, and you could only get somebody out by knocking them down with the ball or a bat. If those were the rules, I guarantee you he would have been a star. Him and Sam Huff and Lieutenant Calley.

On the other end of the spectrum, Francis was a baseballer by birth. His main problem was he didn't have much of an arm. But he was fast afoot and made an okay second baseman. Batting, though, he never could figure out what those breaking balls were doing. I never could stop him from doing a little hula dance up at the plate while he was deciding whether to swing, bail out, or go blind.

But I also knew from an early age their hearts weren't in it, and they played baseball because they felt like I wanted them to. And I did. I'm not going to sit here and tell you different. I've coached high school baseball for twenty years. From the time I finished coaching Little Jackson prematurely until the time my two boys got old enough for high school, I dreamed every day how great it was going to be for all of us to get out of the house and be together all summer at the ball park. Just us guys. No kneeling or praying except in the on-deck circle. But it didn't turn out to be what you'd call a pleasant family experience. Knuck would get frustrated and take it out on Francis every chance he got. And Francis was a walking time bomb.

They exploded simultaneously in public this past summer in Legion ball. Francis was supposed to give Knuck a ride to a game across town at Ambrose P. Hill Field. It got to be a couple of minutes before the game and Knuck still hadn't showed up so I asked Francis if he knew where Knuck was. Francis said he had forgot to pick him up. I asked him, "What do you mean you forgot to pick him up? He lives in the room next to yours."

Well, Francis knows he's in big trouble if he doesn't get Knuck there fast, so he grabs my keys and starts running towards my station wagon in the parking lot. At the same time, here comes Knuck trotting in from the same parking lot having part run and part hitchhiked across town to the game. The two boys run up on one another right there at the bull pen.

Without even so much as a word being exchanged, they go to throwing haymakers and wrestling around in the dirt like a couple of Jap-movie dinosaurs, all in front of a hundred cheering fans who had bought tickets to a high school baseball game, but were being treated to a preliminary prize fight as a bonus.

The boys looked like a couple of cinnamon-covered donuts by the time I could pry them apart with my fungo. They both said they wouldn't play if the other one did. I said to Knuck I hated to break it to him, but he hadn't started all season and what he was proposing wasn't much of a threat. He said he was quitting once and for all and started walking home. But before he left the park and before the fans had stopped gawking, he turned around and shouts at Francis, "You're adopted!"

Francis, the team, and all the people in the stands turned and looked at me, waiting for an answer. I said to Francis, "No, you're not, son. Little Jackson was, but, like it or not, you and Knuck are blood brothers. I checked your birth certificates the last time the two of you combined for no hits in thirteen at bats in a double header." If they hadn't been related to me, I swear I would have traded them both for a decent relief pitcher.

Why Knuck would have used that remark to try to hurt Francis, I couldn't figure. But it made me start wondering had I treated Little Jackson any different.

Well, Francis played out the rest of the season, but he was there in body only. I couldn't for the life of me talk Knuck into coming back out. He made a big point of throwing all his baseball stuff in the trashcan: glove, bat, cleats, everything. After a week or so, Knuck said he wasn't mad any more but that he really needed to start working out more for football. Like he needed more muscles. What he really started doing was drifting further and further away.

Later this past summer, right before school started, Knuck got on this kick about wanting to join the Marines since he was now eighteen. I figured it was a way to gig me. He knew how I felt about war. He made a point of letting me know without really saying so directly that I couldn't stop him. The only thing holding him back, he said, was that he couldn't decide whether to play his final year of high school ball then go play for the Razorbacks and pull the wings off of Southwest Conference quarterbacks or skip his senior year altogether, join the Green Berets, and go kill gooks in Vietnam. How's that for ambition?

I more than once tried to discourage him by telling him about my stint as a prisoner of war in the Pacific, but it wasn't any use. You tell one of these kids today, "Here, son, this hole in my chest is where, when I was your age, they cut my heart out and stomped on it," and he says, "Gee, Dad, that's tough. Please move, you're blocking the TV. It's my favorite *Gilligan's Island*. The one where they try to figure out how to get rescued."

Luckily, I was able to talk Knuck into bringing Francis with him when he went down to the local Marine recruiter's office. That turned out to be a stroke of real genius on my part. Francis told me the recruiters showed them a short movie starring two handsome Marines in their dress blues riding around Paris in a yellow Vette with curvy, barefooted French girls chasing them down curvy brick streets. I'm proud to say that before the movie was over, with a little instructional elbowing and winking from Francis, even Knuck could smell a Tom Sawyering and the boys were able to stiff-arm their way out past the recruiters without getting shanghaied.

Even at that, I worried just as much about Francis as I did Knuck. Maybe more. Francis still tried too hard to be good. Every kid has a water tower of some sort to get away from the things he can't handle. Some water towers are real, others are between the ears. Both serve the same purpose. But as time goes by, the mental water towers get harder and harder to climb down off of, and if you ever slip and fall, chances of survival are slimmer.

But I had both my boys for one last season, although it was football and I was just an' assistant coach. The season started about the middle of August, and the boys had no choice but to spend three or four hours a day within earshot of me. Football isn't an elective at Nathan Bedford Forrest High School, thanks to Coach Grote. Not if you got two legs, two arms, don't look too good in a mini-skirt, and can hold a blocking dummy. It wasn't like my boys and me were doing a lot of communicating, but at least I knew they weren't driving around Paris in a yellow Vette. Or molesting fruit at the supermarket.

Just as I started to feel good about being able to coach both my sons again for what I knew would be one last time, Francis comes to me after the first week of two-a-days and says he wants to quit the team. Great. The Fielder flee reflex kicking in again.

I gave him the first three minutes of the talk I've been giving five or six boys each August for the last nineteen seasons. About two-a-days being tougher than Marine boot camp, and this making a man out of him, and if he can just get past the first two weeks of summer practice, he'd be able to do anything he put his mind to for the rest of his life. Boot camp propaganda. But Francis stops me short and tells me his problem is not that practice is tough, it's that he doesn't want to take a shower.

You coach kids long enough, you learn to take most everything in stride, but I have to admit there was a long dead space before I cleared my head and finally told him, "Francis, you've been hanging around in locker rooms with me since before you could pee standing up. You've seen more naked boys than an Army doctor. You know you don't have nothing to be bashful about. Everyone's got the same basic parts. It's just that looking straight down on things from a height, they always seem smaller. I learned that in the Army Air Corps. It's psychology. What happens if, God forbid, you get drafted and sent to Vietnam? The Army isn't going to build you your own shower stall."

Then he says to me, "But that's what I'm trying to tell you, Jaxdad. I don't think they'd let somebody like me into the Army."

I asked him, "Boys that don't take showers?"

He says, "No, Jaxdad, I can't shower."

"Why?" I says, messing up his hair and trying to grin, "Afraid your waterworks is going to shrink?"

"No," he says, "I'm afraid I'm going to kill somebody. Every night I have a dream that the whole team is in the shower and someone says something to make me mad. Then me and him start to fight in the shower, buck naked. I pound this guy's head into the tiles until it starts to just dissolve into blood like red cotton candy does in your mouth. He quit fighting back a long time ago, but I keep swinging, breaking bones with every punch. Finally, I grab him around the throat and his head comes off in my hands and so the kid bleeds to death there in the shower with me trying to hide this thing behind my back so nobody knows what I did."

Longer dead space.

I took a deep breath and tried for a minute to figure out just what it was he was trying to tell me. A lot of things ran through my head, none of them good. I told him that what he was experiencing was just a natural growing-up thing and it wasn't nothing to worry about. Between you and me, the picture of him foaming at the mouth chained to a hospital bed in a straightjacket come shooting through my brain filter more than once.

He asked me if I knew what the Bible says about such things. I told him I didn't care what the Bible says about it, and he shouldn't either. I reminded him that the Bible says Noah took the animals on the ark two by two, then later on says it was seven by seven. It gives us the Ten Commandments, one of which says, "Thou shalt not kill," and on the very next page the Bible says, "If a man attacks another, kill him." So what it says all depends what page you're on.

I also told him it was best he should shower at home for the time being. I made it clear that he wasn't quitting the team. This Fielder family fleeing had to stop. It was getting us nowhere but gone.

I told him we'd talk about it some more later, but we never did.

7

There's only two ways around violence that I've been able to find: laughing it off and fleeing. Unfortunately, kids can't just walk away from their parents. My kids did have some luck though with humor. That's if you find practical jokes humorous. Some, like my wife, don't.

As soon as we moved to our new house, Dixie removed the wet bar and replaced it with a custom-made shrine to the Blessed Virgin. Bear in mind, this is in addition to the St. Francis of Assisi birdbath shrine she had installed, which is such a stylish accent to my overgrown front yard.

This indoor shrine had enough candles to turn the ceiling gray every few months. In the center was an eighteen-inch plaster statue of the Blessed Virgin Mary next to an eight-by-ten pinup of the Pope. She even rigged up a little padded board to kneel on while she said the rosary. And, eventually, she parked my ball-game-watching recliner in front of it so when she fell asleep praying, she wouldn't fall face first into the candles and go up to heaven in a puff of holy smoke.

A couple of months ago, about two or three weeks into the season, Knuck was fooling around with a football near the shrine bar one afternoon after school, and he broke the head off the statue of Mary. Well, by the way Dixie carried on, you'd have thought he'd decapitated the Archbishop of Cranberry. He got a spanking, a couple of pages of saint stats to learn, and was ordered to spend his measly life savings to replace the statue.

There was a little bookstore and souvenir shop at the Catholic school where the boys attended catechism. Knuck went there looking for another Virgin. The eternal quest.

The old, semiretired nun who ran the store was so excited about a pimply-faced teenager wanting a statue of Mary, she gave him a special inventory reduction deal: two virgins for the price of one. Knuck figured this was a good deal too, because it was like buying insurance for the next time he rolled out in the general direction of the Pope and wrecked the shrine bar.

The two statues of the Virgin Mary that Knuck bought were pretty much identical. I'm sure they were lovingly crafted by the same Japanese indentured servant. The only difference was that one Mary was looking down at her folded hands, the other Mary was looking up to heaven. Knuck gave the looking-up Mary to Dixie and hid the looking-down Mary in his closet, like I said, for insurance.

Dixie said she was pleased with the replacement Mary and took the statue the next morning to church to have it blessed or dunked in holy water or appraised. Whatever they do. I could tell she liked it because she bought a dozen more cathedral-sized candles to beef up the shrine bar. Just what we needed. Just what my ceiling needed. Already I could have barbecued a goat above it.

I honestly don't know how I get fire insurance.

It was about two weeks before the miracles commenced.

The first sign we had that the new replacement statue might have supernatural powers was one night Dixie waking up all three of us to ask whether the Blessed Virgin Mary had been looking up or looking down when we had last seen her. Francis and Knuck agreed, with a surprising amount of certainty, that it was looking up. I was mad that she woke me up for something like that and told her I had thought it was a statue of Elvis she had been praying to all this time and that its head bobbed up and down on a spring.

She insisted that we all come to the shrine bar to witness a bona fide religious miracle, probably the first ever in the Little Rock metropolitan area. To hear it explained by Dixie, sometime during the night while Dixie was sleeppraying, Mary's neck got weary too from the weight of the problems of the world, but instead of falling off her pedestal into the candle furnace, Mary evidently decided to rest her plaster neck by looking down. It was definitely a sign from God that something terrible was about to happen in the world. I said, "Yeah, I'm about to lose an hour's sleep."

I was too tired and my head was too big for me to be born again but Francis and Knuck made a big deal out of it. So much so that I was surprised at them, especially as to Knuck. The boys stayed up talking and praying with Dixie the rest of the night.

The next afternoon I came home from practice and found the whole Women-Who-Wish-They-Would-Have-Been-Born-Men-So-They-Could-Be-Pope Club, all sitting in my den, staring at the looking-down Mary, whispering with Irish accents they learned off of a Bing Crosby movie, and fingering rosary beads as the smoke billowed from enough candles to light the Vatican runway. These women think they've got an inside track to heaven because they've been given "Top Sacred" clearance by the Monsignor and can go in back of the altar.

Sitting in there amongst the Club like they belonged were Francis and Knuck. Now Francis I could understand: but not Knuck. I began to suspect something was up, but I didn't say anything. Not yet.

Well, despite the round-the-clock vigil, nothing miraculous happened for a few more days, and the Women-Who-Would-Be-Pope Club was doing some silent doubting, I'm sure, because most of them had quit occupying my living room and had gone back to hanging out at the church vestry -- whatever that is. Then another miracle happened, this time one morning right after me and the kids left for school. The Virgin Mary raised her head and was now looking up again.

Back came the Women-Who-Would-Be-Pope Club and now they were deadly serious. They took over my house completely. The only good things about the invasion were that, first, my toilet seat stayed warm twenty-four hours a day. Second, I got my ball-game-watching recliner back temporarily because they had to move it to make way for more folding chairs around the shrine bar. And lastly, they brought plenty of donuts. Church women live on donuts and coffee, if you don't know. The biblical name for *donut* is *manna*. Me and the kids ate donuts for breakfast and supper for a week. If it hadn't been for school lunches, we would have got nary a vitamin at all. As it was, we were beginning to show the first signs of rickets. But they were bound and determined to stay till they all witnessed the miracle or proved it a hoax, one.

See, it turns out there was a little tension amongst the Club members. Trouble in paradise. Dixie knew a little too much of the Old Testament. Some of the women found that admirable. Another faction found it highly suspicious. I didn't know this until they invaded my house. It's amazing what you can learn during commercials just sitting there in your own recliner.

During that week-long vigil, there were quite a few arguments and some near hair pullings among the Women-Who-Wish Club. Every two or three hours, just as they'd start nodding off, one of them would shout out, "Alleluia! She moved!" and scare the holy water out of the others. Then they'd get to accusing one another of making it up just so they'd seem holier than the others, who were obviously holier than the one who last saw it move. They even called the Monsignor on the phone a couple of times to keep a full-fledged donnybrook from breaking out. I got to enjoying this so much, I swiveled my ball-game-watching recliner away from the TV and began spending all my spare time watching the Club spar around the shrine bar.

One night, while Dixie was bathing or tuning her rosary or something, the meanest looking of all the Women-Who-Would-Be-Pope -- me and the boys just called her "the one with the moustache" -- she started whispering and some of her cronies picked up the statue and messed with the bottom of it. Out of the corner of my eye, I saw they were doing something but acted like I was watching "Gunsmoke."

Later that night I told Francis and Knuck to get in the car, we needed some ice cream. Vitamin D and calcium. I told them what the one with the moustache had done and that I figured the women had put some kind of a secret mark on the bottom so that they could tell if some pagan was swapping statues on them. Neither of the boys said a thing. They acted like they didn't hear me, but in the rear-view mirror, I saw them whispering and could tell they were worried about the latest developments.

The next day Francis asked me could he borrow nine dollars, which I knew from what Knuck had told me to be the price of one eighteen-inch plaster Blessed Virgin Mary. I told him I would spot him the money but only if he answered me one question: "You going to buy a looking-up or looking-down Mary?"

He tried hard not to smile for a couple of seconds, but it was no use. His mouth finally cracked and we laughed for ten minutes. He said that the one with the moustache had written her name on the bottom of the looking-up Mary with a black Marks-a-Lot. Him and Knuck were going to buy another looking-up Mary and try to substitute it for the marked one so they could copy the name onto the looking-down Mary. I told him that the nine dollars was my treat and to count me in. He said they might could use an extra hand and the three of us got another cone full of nutrients and made plans. This was better than "Mission Impossible." I can't tell you how proud I was of my boys. Finally, working together for a good cause.

When we got home, there were the usual half-dozen assorted cars parked in front of our house, all with a statue of St. Christopher on the dash. The boys walked in first, nonchalantly, and took a couple of the cheap seats at the shrine bar. I came in unnoticed a couple of minutes later, huffed and puffed, and blew my coach's whistle as hard as I ever have. Rosaries flew everywhere.

I announced to the Women-Who-Would-Be-Pope Club that I didn't care if the statue was drinking cheap wine out the bottle while doing the hully-gully, I wanted them out of my house. I put on the same face I've been using for two decades to scare my players into thinking I was ready to clean house. They started to break camp, grabbing for missals and handbags and shuffling for the door, one behind the other, like a gray flannel caterpillar. Dixie slipped in front and asked them in her Catholic accent to excuse the two of us for a wee moment.

Dixie took me out to the garage and conceded that the last few weeks had undoubtedly been hard on me and the boys but this was something great and wonderful and holy, like Lourdes or Fatima or South Bend. She also pointed out the non-spiritual benefits: hadn't we gotten to eat donuts for weeks? She begged me to let the women stay. She squeezed my arm. It was a squeeze with some love in it.

I wanted to take advantage of this momentary thaw to talk with her about our miserable lives, but I never got the chance. She was only concerned about her miracle.

I tried to look at the bright side. At least I had a small part to play in what could turn out to be one of the top ten practical jokes of all time. If we played this thing right, the Pope hisself might someday be sitting in my recliner, eating donuts and making up new prayers for Our Lady of Little Rock.

I hemmed and hawed, stalling for a little time, but finally I told her they could stay.

The next morning at breakfast the boys came up to me sitting at the kitchen table and gave me the thumbs-up sign. Mission impossible accomplished. I ringed a couple of donuts on their thumbs, and we drove to school laughing like we never had before.

It took a few more days before the boys could switch the looking-down Mary with the forged signature for the looking-up Mary with the real signature. They did it in the middle of the night during one of the Club's many bathroom-stuffing, donut-popping, knee-rubbing breaks.

I knew something had happened when I heard the first scream and the fold-up chairs banging around, followed by a loud crash and some crying. I decided not to get out of bed or else it might look suspicious, and was fixing to die of curiosity when I heard still more screaming, doors slamming, and cars burning rubber out of my driveway.

It turns out that when the Club discovered Mary had looked down again, the head one with the moustache bullied her way to the front of the shrine bar and turned over the statue. Seeing her name on the bottom, or a reasonable facsimile thereof, the dainty thing acted like she was going to faint and in the process slung the Blessed Virgin across the room. When she hit the floor, she exploded into mostly powder.

While half the Club was busting a gut trying to hold the one with the moustache aloft, the other half was trying to forcibly restrain Dixie who, by this time, was punting fold-up chairs trying to get to the shrine-bar. I got no doubt in my mind she would have ripped that moustache off the woman's lip if they would have let her loose.

A couple of women fanned the mustached lady with their missals and asked her if her name was still on the bottom. First, she said yes. Then she said she wasn't sure. Then Dixie accused her of atheism and of dropping the statue on purpose. Everybody said everybody else was going to roast in hell and before somebody could get the Monsignor on the phone, one of the women slapped another and it was nip-and-tuck as to whether all heck was going to break out. But it didn't. After some pretty sophisticated cussing and finger wagging, half of the ladies left while the other half sifted through the rubble until it was conceded that Elmer's glue wasn't going to be enough to solve the greatest theological mystery since the Immaculate Conception.

Early the next morning, Dixie and one of the Women-Who-Would-Be-Pope brought the statue crumbs for the Monsignor to examine. Poor fellow. He really isn't a bad guy. I told him one time after mass that I suspected he was married. Otherwise, he couldn't make hell sound so real in his sermons. He laughed. I don't know what he told Dixie and the other ladies, but they came back with a brand new statue of St. Jude and a candle big around as a hundred-pound bomb.

When the boys came down for breakfast, there was only three donuts left. One for each of our thumbs. Even a day old, that was the best donut I ever ate.

When Dixie had squeezed my arm in the washroom the night before, it reminded me of the last vacation we took before we found out Rosie was sick. We rented a cabin at Hot Springs just before school started. One night after the kids had gone to sleep, Dixie and I were on the porch, lying together in the hammock. Without me asking, she told me how I was her knight in armor who had ridden into her life and saved her, a poor damsel in distress. She said she never thought she could love anyone as much as Jugs, but she loved me more. I can close my eyes and still smell her hair. I think that was the happiest evening of my life.

But now, most of the happy days I have are in spite of Dixie. The most pitiful thing about her lately is that it's so rare when she laughs. When she does, no matter why, both boys go run to her like puppies and hug on her hoping, I guess, that this is a sign that the ice age is over.

The last time I can remember her laughing real hard was not too long ago when I announced to the family at the supper table that I was thinking about going back to school to get a master's degree in physics. She enjoyed that. She give out with a real horse laugh.

The closest thing Dixie had to a friend, not counting the saints, the priests, and the women she hung out with who wanted to be saints and priests, was young Andy Johnson from down the street. Andy was a great big kid Knuck's age who was being raised, sort of, by his father and older brothers. He started coming around our house because his home life wasn't very stable. You know if he wanted to hang around our happy incubator, his home had to really stink. But I never saw him without a smile except when I had to tell him it was time to go home.

I'll give you a recent example of Andy's pitiful existence. One afternoon after football practice, I offered Andy a ride home. He asked me to drop him off about a block away from his house. After he got out of the car, I asked the boys what that was all about. Knuck told me matter-of-factly that he had to go dig up his doll. Francis explained that Mr. Johnson, Andy's father, was disappointed Andy wasn't getting more playing time during the football games and Johnson, along with Andy's big brothers, had taken to addressing him as Angelica and making him carry a doll to school.

Andy was the kind of kid that tried a little too hard to make the other kids like him. He was always good for a laugh at his own expense. At lunch he'd be the guy to spray milk out of his nose at even the hint of something funny. They'd be standing around in a crowd of boys and girls, and somebody would say something about his breasts being bigger than some poor girl standing next to him. He'd laugh and act the fool. You've got to be desperately lonely if you'd be the butt of the jokes rather than get left out.

Andy was Baptist, and him and Dixie would talk for hours about the finer points of Bapto-Catholicism, like mortal sin, venial sin, and original sin. He was always worried, since he hadn't been baptized Catholic, whether he would be going to heaven or hell or purgatory or limbo or the Congo. Wherever. Dixie would have liked nothing better than to have scared him into converting to Catholicism.

He was always asking her about guardian angels and would really light up when Dixie told him that he had one too, even though he was a Baptist and was quickly getting too old for limbo. Andy's goal in life, besides being officially recognized by the Little Rock City Board as the village idiot, was to some day become a Catholic like Dixie.

I couldn't tell if Andy was really interested in

converting or just wanted Dixie to like him. She was the closest thing to a mother he had. Come to think of it, she was the closest thing to a mother my boys had.

I thought seriously several times about trying to convert him to Einsteinism, but figured if between me and Gale Sayers we couldn't figure out the theory of relativity, adding Andy to the congregation wasn't going to get us no further along. In fact, it would drop the congregation's collective I.Q. considerably.

I remember when I noticed for the second time Andy coming over with a black eye. He was the least likely person I know to have gotten in a fight, so I asked him what happened. He said he fell down his front steps. I know he didn't want to tell me the truth, so I let it go. Later Knuck told me Andy's father beats all the brothers and all the brothers beat Andy. And who do you think Andy's father is? None other than Steel Mill Johnson, the supposed victim in this whole deal. He's the reason one of my boys is dead and the other one locked up. Some victim.

8

Before I hit forty, I told myself that if I could just keep my arm healthy, something would happen to get me back in the major leagues. I played pitch and catch with Little Jackson and my other kids as much for me as for them. Maybe another war would come along where, this time, I would be one of the 4Fs who got to stay home and play professional ball. But they don't have wars anymore, just police actions and such.

So for the last seven years since forty tolled, I've just been marking the time till I die with one ball season after another that don't mean nothing in the grand scheme of things, if there even happens to be a grand scheme of things. I thought having my younger boys, Knuck and Francis, play for me would put some emotion back in my life, but the pre-game hype was too much for the boys to live up to. And they played in spite of me, not because of me.

Then I got the interim head football coaching job, and one Friday night at a time, winning the state championship somehow became the most important thing in my life. The championship comes with fringe benefits. Besides somewhat justifying the last twenty years and earning the respect of my sons, it usually also means an offer to go coach at a college somewhere. It became my ejection seat out of this crippled flying fortress I've made of my life.

My boys playing for me plus the chance of the three of us sharing a state championship had me so excited I was ready to sell my soul to get that trophy and get myself out of purgatory. But the devil wanted more than my soul. He wanted my boys. All three of them. All I got.

I don't know if you follow high school football, but 1969 was supposed to be the year of the Horsemen. Preseason, Nathan Bedford Forrest High was ranked number one in the state. We had sixteen starters coming back and almost all our skill-position players returning. Last year, you might remember, we had made it to the state semifinals but the team got wiped out by the flu bug. We got beat 56 to 6 by a team we should have been able to beat with neither chin nor jock straps.

Last week the boys made it through the semifinals as barely as you can and still get there. And now all this. Some of the Horse Backers had the nerve to come up to me at the cemetery this afternoon and ask me whether we were going to have practice tomorrow or whether the team was going to have to play Friday's state championship game with no preparation at all. They *did* have the courtesy to wait until after the Monsignor had closed his prayerbook.

Just so you know, the Horse Backers are a club, more like a gang, of arm-chair quarterbacks whose two main goals in life are to get for their sons the football scholarships they never had and to make the head coach's life as close to hell-on-Earth as possible. They do a lot better at the latter.

It's a sad state of affairs when the only living you do is through your kids. I know. For one thing, the rules for keeping them in line stop working when fathers get too involved because the referees are now playing the game, so to speak. They're all teammates and everyone acts the worst for it: fathers and sons.

The president of the Horse Backers is Mr. Steel Mill Johnson. That's right. Him. Steel Mill supposedly played pro football for some midwest mining town that hasn't had a movie theater, much less a pro football team, since way before the war. He's been living off the legend of his legend for years. If he wasn't a giant and mean as a snake, no one would listen to a word he says. I can't believe the police would believe him over my boy.

My boys told me he keeps his football trophies in a trophy case right by the front door so you can't help but ask about them when you walk into his house. Which, by the way, is the only thing about his house that you could possibly admire.

The Johnsons' house is on our block. There are always no less than seven junked cars in the front yard, every one without tires, stranded up on cinder blocks. It's where old, rusty cars go to die. The roof of their house is covered with branches that have been there for decades. Little saplings are growing out of what's left of their gutters. I bet it's the only pitched roof in the world that has a basketball stuck on it. The whole estate is guarded by a big black dog chained to a tree in the front yard, like someone was going to sneak off with their treasure.

Like me, Steel Mill had himself three boys. Unlike me, he still has three. All ugly as dirt dobbers' nests. He nurtured them with an iron fist instead of a mother. I had the displeasure of coaching them all, I'm sorry to say. The two older boys were strong and mean like their father, and one of them may have eventually played junior college ball for a year or two somewhere. But size and intelligence never were their strong suits, and if they can land a job at the scrap-iron yard with their dad, they will have reached their full potential, I swear.

Andy was the only Johnson son to hang around my boys. Andy was the youngest and biggest of the three Johnson brothers. Old Coach Grote, who had seen thirty-five crops of kids come through Little Rock high schools, had been drooling for at least two years waiting for Steel Mill Johnson's third boy -- "the big one" -- to put on the black and white. Me, I knew better. Andy had been at my house seeking sanctuary and talking guardian angels with my wife every day since he was a little sinner, and I knew for him to be a good football player, God would pretty much have to drop everything else he had planned for several years.

The Johnson family was famous several months ago about the time school started. For whatever reason, maybe to replace their mom, Johnson bought his boys a real live monkey. Talk was he won it off a tugboat captain in a crap game.

They built the monkey a scrap-metal cage in their backyard. For a while, every kid within ten miles was spending his afternoons at the Johnsons' house, watching the monkey do monkey things. But after a couple of weeks, the new wore off and the smell didn't, so the poor monkey was all but abandoned. Like Andy.

The job of feeding the little ape and hosing down his

cage rolled downhill, or maybe up the evolutionary ladder, from Steel Mill, past the two Cro-magnon boys, and finally stopped at Andy. And Andy didn't appreciate getting stuck with yet another job just because his brothers were older and meaner.

Andy took his pent-up anger out on the poor monkey, throwing his food at him, spraying him with the hose every chance he got and poking him through the bars of his cage with the manure-rake handle. They developed a love-hate relationship. Andy loved to torment the poor monkey and the monkey hated Andy's fat behind.

It all came to a head one Sunday afternoon in late Septempber. Andy was hosing off the monkey when all of a sudden the monkey, who had evidently taught himself how to pick the latch on the cage door, came flying out of the cage and, with the strength of Mighty Joe Young, latched onto Andy's head and started gnawing on his ear. Only God knows what would have happened if Andy had been fifty pounds lighter or if the Johnson brothers hadn't heard the commotion and counter attacked. It took the hose full blast and a couple of well placed shots with the manure-rake to get the monkey to turn loose. I remember Dixie making some joke about the keeper's brothers being their brother's keeper. Nothing flatter in my book than a bad religious joke. I'm sure she had the church women rolling in the aisles with that stinker.

That night, when Steel Mill got home from the scrap metal yard, his older boys told him about the unprovoked ape ambush. He ate the supper Andy had fixed him without saying a word. The boys watched him carefully for some hint of what he was going to do. They knew it was going to be bad for somebody. They were just hoping it wasn't everybody.

When he had finished his sandwiches, without saying a word Johnson pushed back from the kitchen table, walked back to Andy's room and, after a few minutes of crashing around in Andy's closet, came back to the kitchen with Andy's 34-inch, Yogi Berra model, Louisville Slugger. Holding the fat part in his giant hand and pointing the handle at Andy's face, he said, "If I had to choose between you and the monkey for a son, I'd pick the monkey. He ain't afraid of his own shadow. And he don't eat as much. But I ain't got that choice. I'm stuck with you. A fat, cry-baby coward. And you remember who it is responsible for what I have to do."

Andy tried to stop him but didn't try as hard as he might have if Steel Mill hadn't had a baseball bat in his hand and hadn't just said what he said. Andy's brothers pushed Andy down on the kitchen floor and told him to shut up.

Steel Mill marched toward the monkey cage with his older boys yipping at his heels like coon dogs. He took some practice swings with the bat trying to get his timing down. He looked more like a neanderthal with a club than a baseball player. Steel Mill was definitely a footballer.

He got about ten feet from the cage and had his head down, showing off for his boys, acting like he was a batter knocking the dirt out of his cleats when the monkey jimmied the latch again and came flying out of the cage headed for Steel Mill's jugular, screeching like the proverbial bat from hell. Steel Mill screamed and turned to run but the monkey wrapped itself around his head like a pea vine on a cyclone fence and started biting him in the face.

The monkey, bless its hairy little heart, was a scrapper and, given another thirty-five pounds, it would have killed Steel Mill for sure or bit off his big red nose, one. But as it was, Steel Mill was finally able to unwrap the monkey from off his face and clobber it with the bat over and over again until it finally quit wiggling.

That's about the time Andy high-tailed it away from the Johnson zoo and over to the Fielder incubator. He was crying and shaking like I never seen before. To see a boy that big with the body of a man as scared as a little kid was a pitiful sight. Me, Dixie, Francis, and Knuck sat around our kitchen table trying to calm him down. We assured him that his father was not going to kill him. But none of us was sure enough ourselves to convince Andy.

About an hour later, Steel Mill called to ask if Andy was over at my house. I said he was. Steel Mill told me that coach or no coach, I should stop trying to interfere with him raising his boy. He said I should concentrate on my own kids, who needed a little discipline themselves. And he told me to tell my wife to quit trying to fill Andy's head with Catholic nonsense or he'd come kick my butt.

I thought about calling Steel Mill out in the street under the Code of the West, but, truth be told, I wouldn't have had a chance in a fair fight. He is a big fellow and, unlike me, still actually has muscles. And the heart of a donut.

I ended up saying I would send Andy home. After all, Andy was his kid. And I had enough problems with raising my own family.

Andy heard me chicken out on the phone and looked at me like I had just stuck a yarmulke on his head and pointed him out to the Gestapo. I knew what he was in for, but I figured, not being kin, I had no legal right to protect the boy from his father. Dixie agreed. The Bible and all that. As he left, my boys gave me the death ray and promised Andy they would help even if I wouldn't. I knew from having raised them from pups that "help" usually meant more like getting even.

Now some of the rest of what I'm going to tell you I know you remember from the news. But I'm sure you probably didn't make the connection that the Mr. Johnson who swore out the complaint against my boy is the same Mr. Johnson whose picture was in every paper in the country last month for trying to pull a hoax on the U.S. Air Force.

The next evening after football practice my boys stayed locked up in the garage. I could hear them shaking spray-paint cans and buzzing my barber shears that I used to give them two-minute crew cuts with when they were little, back before the Beatles. But I left them alone. I could tell they were on a mission. They had that look in their eyes, one I hadn't seen in the mirror for quite a few years.

About ten o'clock, I knocked on the garage door and told them they needed to go to bed. There was dead quiet for a second, then some scurrying, then they opened the door just a crack. They started pleading with me, nothing specific, just saying they couldn't go to bed. They had something very important to do and they couldn't quit just yet. I told them to be in the kitchen in five minutes to plead their case.

They were a little late. They reeked of gasoline and in the kitchen light they had a silver sheen to their eyebrows and hair. I figured they had been using the gasoline to clean the silver spray paint off themselves the best they could. I lectured them on the dangers of spontaneous combustion, especially with all the lit candles in our house.

I asked them point blank what they were up to. They said they couldn't tell me but they were going to help Andy. I said that wasn't good enough, they had to tell me what they were doing. They asked me to trust them. They said it was a matter of life and death. I just hoped they weren't planning on killing Steel Mill. Now I can't imagine ever hoping that.

I don't know why, but I decided to take a chance. I could tell they were desperate and if they could figure out how to help Andy, more power to them. I hadn't done a lick of good for him so far, and I'm his coach and a veteran. I settled in to watch the *Tonight Show* and wait for the boys to come home.

About midnight, there was a flash that lit up the whole house followed by an explosion that knocked me out of my ball-game watching recliner. It sounded like a string of hundred pounders dropped from a B-29. After I remembered that World War II was over, my next thought was that the boys had blown theirselves up in the garage. I stumbled into the kitchen half asleep and ran into Dixie coming in from the shrine bar. I opened the back door and was greatly relieved to find the garage still attached to my house, but the sky was lit up to the west. Knuck was on the phone to the police reporting, in his deepest disc-jockey voice, that a meteorite or something had crashed down the street in the Johnson's back yard. A meteorite? I wondered how he could know such a thing within a matter of seconds but I let it go. Without a doubt, something big had happened and I wanted to see what it was.

Dixie and I grabbed our robes and slippers and headed out the door. Along the way, we met up with the rest of the neighborhood dressed in their robes and slippers doing the same thing. Nothing like a good outer-space invasion to bring a neighborhood closer together.

When we got to the Johnsons', it was clear from the distribution of neighbors and the red glow from behind the house that whatever there was to see was in their back yard. Steel Mill's rabid hound-from-hell kept the neighbors from passing through the front yard, so they were hopping chain-link fences trying to get around back of the house. Even Dixie scaled a four-foot brick wall without too much trouble. Boosting her up and over, we laughed like we had as kids back in Smackover. But she was preoccupied. She was miracle hunting.

We got to the backyard at the same time as the first fire hoses and just ahead of the police dogs. It was the most bizarre scene I ever saw this side of wartime Japan. Straight out of the "Twilight Zone." There was a ring of fire in the middle of the backyard, about twenty feet across. In the middle of the fire there was a five-foot-wide ring of grass that wasn't yet burned. In the middle of the grass ring was a little crater. And lying in the middle of the crater was a silver something or somebody that nobody could quite make out through the flames. The flames reflecting off this thing's shiny surface made it look like it was moving.

From my spot at the fence, I could see Steel Mill, who was in his underwear, trying to untangle himself from his garden hose, band-aids all over his face. I'd seen Steel Mill Johnson a thousand times. He had a bad habit of coming to most football practices and pointing out the weaknesses of our other defensive tackles hoping it would elevate Andy's stock. Until this night, I never saw him when his jaw wasn't jutting out like he was walking into a gale. This night, all he had was just a quivering, boneless chin. Whatever or whoever it was in the circle of flames had him spooked.

Before the fire hoses got completely rolled out and connected, one of the firemen yelled that the thing in the middle of the circle was a child and it was alive and to stand back, he was going in after it. The crowd held its breath. Dixie crossed herself. The fireman wrapped a fire blanket around himself, got a running start, and, even in his waders, covered the ten feet of flames in less than a second, without any regard for his own life.

He bent down in the circle of grass for a split second like he was going to scoop the child up out of the little crater, but before you could say "Martian," he slung off his blanket and came flying back out through the circle of fire faster than he went in, leaving the silver whatever-it-was where it lay.

And he didn't slow down when he cleared the flames neither. He kept on trucking. I guess the other firemen thought by his incoherent screaming and the expression of bug-eyed terror on his face that he had caught himself on fire, because they ran him down from behind, tackled him, and smothered him with blankets. But even though he never had been on fire, he wouldn't quit screaming. Shrieking was more like it. The whole crowd was spooked now, me included.

About then is when they hit the circle of flames with the fire hoses and put the fire out in pretty short order. I wondered why they didn't just go and get the aluminum child or whatever it was out of the center of the circle right away, but they didn't. There was a lot of shining of flashlights and talking on walkie-talkies, but the firemen and the police kept a healthy distance.

A jet fighter flew over at treetop level. Steel Mill's junkyard dog led the police dogs baying at the moon. The hair stood up straight on the back of my neck. I saw a couple of cops checking their guns to make sure they were loaded.

Then the neighbors nearest the firemen started shouting. Some of the weaker at heart began high-tailing it for home, hurdling fences. Word spread along the fence faster than the Hong Kong flu until it finally got to us. The silver thing was an honest-to-god spaceman. A spaceman had crashlanded in Little Rock, Arkansas. In our neighborhood. But he was dead and now there would be the Martians to pay, sure as Ming the Merciless wears a big collar. Everyone had seen enough Martian movies to know this was a bad omen.

Dixie stopped crossing herself only long enough to vault back over the brick wall, no help needed. She was scrambling for home. I got caught up in the panic myself and started calling for Knuck and Francis to take them to our neighbor's bomb shelter.

I finally found them up in a tree in the yard next to the Johnsons', laughing like a couple of gassed hyenas. I coaxed them down with a promise of complete amnesty. I knew my boys well enough just by looking at them not to go beg my neighbor for a corner of his bomb shelter.

Not just yet.

It turns out that after Steel Mill killed the monkey with the baseball bat, Knuck and Francis snuck the dead critter out of the trash can, shaved it, snipped off its tail with my garden shears, and then spray painted it silver, head to toe and everything in between. They laid it down in a hole they dug in the middle of the Johnsons' back yard and poured ten gallons of gasoline in a circle around it, but far enough away that it wouldn't burn the monkey for some time. Finally, they sprinkled a gross of cherry bombs in and around the gasoline circle so that the cherry bombs would all go off pretty much within a couple of seconds after they put a match to the ring of gasoline. It was Son of Ray Bob.

The boys' plan to get even with Steel Mill couldn't have worked better if the man from U.N.C.L.E. had planned it hisself. The Air Force bomb squad picked the galactic traveler up off the ground using a remote control arm and stuck it in an air-tight capsule of some kind. An ambulance followed by half a dozen police cars took the silver spaceman to the coroner's office, sirens and lights blaring, with all the TV news camera trucks not far behind. Another police car took Steel Mill, still in his underwear, to the police station to be questioned by some Air Force intelligence officers who had been helicoptered in from the nearest SAC base with orders to save planet Earth at all costs, or at least Washington.

By morning, the autopsy showed the spaceman to be a mere undernourished South American spider monkey who had had its head caved in by a blunt object some time before it was shaved, de-tailed, spray painted, and partially barbecued. Steel Mill pleaded ignorance, but he was convicted of cruelty to animals and sentenced to three days in the county jail. The seventy-two hours he spent locked up were Andy's happiest three days since before his mother skipped out on them ten years ago with a professional bowler, looking for life in the fast lane.

The day he got out of jail, Steel Mill made a point of catching me after football practice. He put his giant hairy finger in my face and told me he knew my boys had something to do with the stupid Martian prank, as he called it, and that he was going to get even someday when I least expected it. He said: "You and your boys ain't so smart as you think you are, big Mister Fairy Baseball Player." I said I was sure he was mistaken, but would certainly talk to my boys just in case.

The more I thought about his threat, the madder I got. I couldn't sleep. I got up in the middle of the night and searched our attic. I was looking to get even. I finally found the stuffed monkey, Mister Mugs, that Rosie used to sleep with. I went out to the garage and spray-painted it silver. Then, it being about two in the morning, I snuck out of the house and walked down the block to the Johnson house.

I got as close to their house as their dog would let me. At that time, the Johnsons had the biggest, meanest, blackest dog you ever saw. They kept it on a chain padlocked to the oak tree out in front of their house, year round. Any time I ever saw that dog it was foaming at the mouth and pulling on the chain like it would maul you if it got half a chance. I don't know how they got close enough to feed it. The dog had long since dug up all the dirt under the oak tree and was living on a spider web of roots. I don't know whether the dog even had a name. The boys around the neighborhood called him the Black Widowmaker.

Even Andy couldn't get close to his own dog, and he had to feed it. When the boys got anywhere near the Johnson's front yard, Widowmaker would chase them away, dragging about thirty foot of rusty chain to the curb. He'd stretch it out off the ground by standing on his back legs growling, barking, and frothing at the mouth like the K-9's at the gates of hell. The sound of the chain being dragged across the roots was worse than a pencil in the ear. My heart would start pumping hard every time I passed by there in a car. And I'm a veteran.

The bottom line was that the dog was mistreated something terrible. Except for the oak tree and the junk cars, he had no shelter, summer nor winter, neither rain nor shine. If he barked for too long, old Steel Mill would come out and swat him with the radio antennae he kept on the front porch for just that purpose.

More than once, Francis asked me wasn't there anything we could do about that poor dog. Me, I was scared of dogs in general and the Black Widowmaker in particular. When I was a little boy, my father told me not to be afraid of a particularly mean-looking dog down the street. He told me when the dog growled, it was just grinning at me. I wasn't afraid for about a week. Then I got too close to the dog and it grinned through the seat of my pants. And, truth be told, I wasn't wild about Steel Mill Johnson or his antennae either. Steel Mill would do more than grin through the seat of my pants if I gave him half an excuse.

So I told Francis he might as well learn now that we couldn't cure all the problems in the world and to just let it be. He asked Dixie about it, and she told him that God told man to have dominion over every living thing that moveth upon the earth or some such platitude. I don't know that I agreed with her but at least it got me out of an awkward situation. The Bible is good for that for sure.

Where was I? Oh, yeah. I got to Steel Mill's house with the silver stuffed monkey, and with the same windup that made me the scourge of the American League during September of 1941, I hurled the stuffed monkey, Son of Son of Ray Bob, clear from the street over the dead car cemetery, over the Black Widowmaker, and onto the Johnson roof, where it rested in peace until yesterday. Fairy Baseball Player, my you-know-what.

A few days after my prank, Francis came to me and confessed he'd accidentally broken my hack saw and he'd bought me a new blade but couldn't figure out how to rig it. I wondered what he had been doing with my saw, but I rigged it up for him anyway and didn't think much more about it. It wasn't a day or so after that that I noticed the Black Widowmaker was AWOL.

The only way Francis could have cut that dog's chain without getting eaten alive was if he had had some help. I suspected maybe it was Andy who helped, wishing he'd be the next one getting set free. And maybe that's my job. To set Andy free from Steel Mill like the boys set the Black Widowmaker free. Or like Steel Mill had set the monkey free.

I didn't realize it then, but another undeclared war was escalating.

9

Andy Johnson was neither a footballer nor a baseballer. He was an oddballer. Playing on his father's nickname, Steel Mill, the kids called Andy "Still-a-mule" and "Steal-a-meal". I'll never forget the time Coach Grote finally got a chance to see Andy up close like I had been seeing him since he was in elementary school. It was a couple of summers ago, before two-a-days started. We had the incoming sophomores in the gym bleachers getting ready to give them their six-second physicals and lay down the ground rules. "Break 'em in early and right," Coach Grote would say.

He gave the same speech to every new bunch of sophomore footballers for the last thirty-five years. It started by saying greatness was not for everybody, nor was hard work. The eventual moral was that if you lived to be a hundred, there would be nothing you could possibly do with your life to top having played on an Arkansas state championship football team. What could be better than to obtain immortality, and as a teenager, no less. It's the same kind of stuff they tell the Kamikazes. Take no prisoners!

Coach Grote had just started the fist-pounding, spit-frothing part of his speech when Andy, who was sitting about halfway up in the bleachers, jumped on his belly down between the benches, which made the sound of two trash trucks colliding, and disappeared under the grandstand. Coach Grote was just as shocked as everyone else, including me, and he stopped talking and waited for Andy to resurface, which he did about ten seconds later. Andy crawled back up through the bleachers, sat down, and dusted himself off. When he saw everybody was looking at him, he held up his hand with something green in it and gave a one word explanation for his behavior: "lizard." Coach Grote stood there silently for a minute while yet another dream evaporated. Then he looked at me and rolled his eyes. That belly flop in the bleachers was the closest Andy Johnson ever got to participating in an athletic event during all the time Coach Grote was in charge.

It wasn't just the lizard safari. Andy was a good-natured kid, but he seemed to be forever crossing Coach Grote. Before we played our first game this season, in addition to the team picture in uniform taken on the bleachers like it'd been done since Knute Rockne was a baby, for some reason Coach Grote had the team show up at the Belmont Motor Hotel in sports coats and ties to get their picture taken on the spiral staircase. I asked Coach Grote what for and he said, "For a change." I know the kids didn't have any better idea as to what was up than I did. I've got to admit we were all curious.

About a week after we took the picture, right before our first game with J.E.B. Stuart High, Coach Grote called Andy into the coach's office. He said he'd heard from reliable sources that Andy had been telling people around town, including players on the other teams, that the picture we took on the spiral staircase was for *Sports Illustrated* and that behind us had been a presumptuous banner saying "1969 Arkansas State Champions". Andy laughed and said he was just having a little fun; that he hadn't meant no harm. Coach Grote didn't think it was funny. Before he gave him three licks with his underwear off, he said, "Listen, dickweed. If you know you've got to go out and kill a bear, there ain't no sense in getting him mad before you even start out after him."

Well, maybe Coach Grote knew what he was talking about, because we lost our first game to J.E.B. Stuart on the road by a touchdown. We jumped offsides on our first play from scrimmage and that might have been the best one we ran all night. The kids were in a good frame of mind it seemed like, but as Coach Grote reminded me after the game, a good frame of mind never stopped anyone at the goal line. It was a tough loss to swallow, considering our pre-season ranking and publicity. The Horse Backers didn't take it very well. Neither did Coach Grote.

The thought of yet another unperfect record so early in the season was almost too much for poor Coach Grote to bear for the thirty-fifth consecutive time. On the long bus ride back from the opener, he started reminiscing and got all maudlin on me. He told me about himself going to school in a cabin in the Pennsylvania mountains. Not at all like Nathan Bedford Forrest High or J.E.B. Stuart High, he said. He studied astronomy through the holes in the roof, geology through the holes in the floor, and anatomy through the hole in the girls' outhouse. He talked until he worked his way through his three-and-a-half decades in high school coaching. Not all too fondly, either. As all the adults back to Adam had done, we agreed that the kids now days didn't know how good they had it.

There was a long pause where I guess he was trying to decide whether he would open up all the way down to the quick. Then he told me for the first time that his nickname was Skink and what had happened to him in the Pacific as a Marine.

He was in an outfit that cleaned up the Jap soldiers after an island had been hopped and declared secure, but before the fighting really stopped. He said they hunted for snipers, which was a more nerve-wracking job even than coaching high school football.

He told me about his outfit sweeping Okinawa. About the third day there, they were hunkered down under a wall when some crazed Jap wanting to kill himself and all of Coach's outfit along with him, screamed like a banshee, tucked a grenade into his stomach, and did a one-and-a-half off the wall into the pile of Marines, right smack on top of Coach Grote. He said there was nothing any of them could do but just cover up and wait for the grenade to go off. When it did, the Jap soldier blew up into a dozen pieces right amongst them, legs, arms, and assorted guts going every which way.

Coach Grote said he was stunned for a minute from the concussion. When he finally got up the nerve to open his eyes and saw a mangled arm lying two or three feet from his face, he started screaming, "I'm hit! Medic, I'm hit!" thinking his own arm had been blown off. After everybody realized that nobody but the crazy Jap was hurt, they laughed all night. He said from then on he was known in the service as Skink Grote, the wonder boy from

Pennsylvania who had grown back an arm blown off by a hand grenade.

Coach Grote laughed loud, then, all of a sudden, he got quiet again. After that, he said quietly, he and the rest of his outfit got a lot less tolerant of the Japanese. Instead of going down into the caves after the Japs and talking them out with Hershey bars, they would just throw in a couple of grenades and, after the explosions, seal the cave shut with concrete. The Japanese that did come out looking to surrender didn't fare much better. He said a lot of the men in his outfit eventually went to cutting off Japanese ears, scalps and other body parts and keeping them as trophies, wearing them on a shoelace around their necks like charms on a bracelet.

I'm sure that before Pearl, Coach Grote wasn't any more interested in killing the Japanese than I was. But that's what Uncle Sam and our mothers and fathers and neighbors asked us to go do. I guess the both of us did it as best we could. Now here we are twenty-five years later trying to raise not only our own kids but other people's kids, too. None of which little darlings has ever so much as missed a meal, much less been on the wrong side of a machine gun. How is somebody like us, who's been through what we have, gonna be able to raise kids? Once you've had to worry a couple of years about staying alive, it's hard to concern yourself with the day-to-day stuff. After a while, it's all day-to-day stuff. Everything, that is, except war. Arkansas Quad-A high school football and war.

I coached with Coach Grote for nineteen years, and that night on the bus was the only time he ever told me anything you could call personal about himself. I was encouraged that maybe he was going to soften up on the boys a little bit. I should have known better.

The Monday after that first game was Labor Day. It had rained all day Sunday, and to show the team he wasn't going to let losing become a habit, he called practice for the holiday, water, mud, and all.

The first thing he did was gather the boys for one of his famous pep talks. After everybody got quiet, he waited for a minute, then held up a football. He made a point of showing it to everyone. He announced: "Men, we're going back to the basics. This is a football. This . . ." He started to go on, but Andy said, "Wait, Coach. Not so fast." There were some snickers, then laughs, then Coach Grote blew a gasket. The sun had come out with a vengeance, and the humidity was at least one hundred percent. Those poor boys practiced three hours, full speed, full pads, full contact, with no water. The kids had the cotton mouth so bad they made hissing noises when they ran.

I don't know how long practice would have gone on for if the kids hadn't started laughing like hyenas and falling flat-out on the ground. We looked up to see Andy, on all fours, helmet off, drinking out of a mud puddle, using his teeth to strain the mosquito larvae. Coach Grote took this as a sign that it may have been time to end practice. Andy got a couple of licks anyway. Underwear up, as I recall.

Coach Grote was from the old school. He was almost as big on pep talks as he was on licks. "Carrot and the stick," he used to tell me. He could flat work those kids into a froth better than a faith-healing, snake-toting, tent-puffing revivalist. And if you ever heard him give a pep-talk you never forgot his trademark -- "Stick!" We had to "Stick it to 'em!" "Stick your helmets through their chests!" "Stick 'em till their mamas hurt!" "Stick! Stick! Stick!" On and on until he'd beller out "Take no prisoners!" and the kids would pretty near kill each other in a forearming frenzy.

No telling how many of Little Rock's innocent children got indoctrinated as warriors by Coach Grote in thirty-five years. There wasn't hardly a week went by when a carload of boys who had played for Coach Grote in seasons long since past didn't ride by the practice field with their bare bottoms hanging out a window, one of them yelling, "Hey, Grote, stick this!" Every time, Coach Grote would do the same thing. He'd look up slowly, wave and smile and say, "Some more of my Horsemen. It appears they've gotten better looking since when they played for me. I'm sure proud of all my boys."

A couple of years ago, Coach Grote started awarding little skull and crossbones decals for the kids to put on their helmets if they scored a touchdown or intercepted a pass or something special. As the season went on, you could spot the better offensive players by the number of skull and crossbones they had stuck to their helmets.

Eventually, to promote contact, as if someone needs to promote contact in football, like promoting drinking at a dog fight, Coach Grote started giving out the decals for what he called a "stick." He never really defined what a "stick" was, but the way he would explain it to the kids before the first game was if, on Saturday morning, when we graded the game films, he was pretty sure the stick*ee* was in the other locker room looking at his waterworks in a jar on the trainer's shelf rather than watching the game films, that was worth a skull and crossbones decal. It wasn't long before those decals became more important to some kids than winning the game. I'm not sure they didn't become more important to Coach Grote too.

One of Coach Grote's regular sermons to me was about how football had gone soft. For a long time, he blamed it on the advent of face masks, and just recently he started blaming foreign-born, soccer-style kickers with long hair. He liked to tell the story about playing football on a frozen tundra somewhere in Pennsylvania or West Virginia and getting kicked in the mouth one time with a steel-toed cleat while trying to block a punt. He said he spit two teeth straight out and pulled a third one out later in the game with his own fingers because it kept cutting into his chapped lip every time he got hit in the chin. But then he'd go on to tell he gave a lot worse than he got and the warm beer after the game healed his gums better than penicillin. Then he'd look up to the ceiling with the same expression on his face as the Apostles in the stained glass windows at the Cathedral and say, "Now *that* was football." And I'd think, "Now, *that* was crazy."

In Smackover, where I'm from, you didn't play organized football until you got to the high school. My brother Jugs was a year older than me, and I watched him quarterback the team for a year before I took a shot at playing. I played for the reason most kids did, I guess, to get that tag after your name: "There's Jackson Fielder. He plays football." I wanted a description behind my name and the instant respect it commanded. There weren't many automatic ones dispensed in our neck of the woods during the Depression: he plays football; his daddy's rich; his daddy's a sot; they're poor as Job's turkey. But we were as solid middle-class as there was in the Depression and my father could hold his liquor, so playing football was the only way I was gonna get me one.

Along with the description, the guys who played football got a little more room, if you know what I mean. If you strayed a little, you were more likely to get a wink than a swift kick. In the days before the war, high school football players were as close to war heroes as we had, especially in Smackover.

To tell you the honest-to-God truth, I never really liked the game of football. I liked wearing all the pads and stuff. But it gave you a false sense of security. I could play a whole summer of baseball without once getting hurt, and I couldn't go through one football practice without something turning black and blue. One problem was that I was puny. I'd go about one-twenty on a Sunday afternoon after lunch, with my head and feet making up maybe two-thirds of that weight.

From first grade to tenth grade, all the boys were verbally committed to going out for varsity football. Of course, you couldn't play till tenth grade, so the early commitment didn't mean much. When tenth grade rolled around, it was time either to join the team or come up with a convincing medical excuse that would let you do everything *but* play football. That summer before tenth grade, there were more made-up pig-latin medical phrases being tossed around Smackover by puny tenth graders-to-be than by all the quacks at the V.A. hospital.

About three weeks into my football career, I decided that, try as I might, I wasn't ever going to be a footballer. This was about a week after the Stonehenge incident I told you about earlier. Seeing what physical contact can do to you, even if you are doing nothing but trying to get out of the way, made me, let's just say, especially cautious.

They had a name for us kids out mainly to get that description after our name, who were too slow to play in the backfield and too light to play on the line. They called us "ends." The old joke was that the coach would chase the team through the woods. The kids that ran around the trees were backs; those that ran into the trees were linemen; those that ran through the trees were linebackers; and those that stop to pick berries were ends. As in "odds and ends." At practice, they sent us ends with the linemen when they needed blocking fodder and with the backs when they needed tackling dummies. We spent a lot of time kneeling on the sidelines trying to look like we had just run a marathon and if it weren't for being dead tired from hustling, we'd just love to go in and let the real footballers knock our buns into our socks.

But that was fine. You got the same description attached to your name regardless of what kind of football player you were or how cautious. No one ever said, "There's Jackson Fielder. He plays football. He'd as soon wear a sarong as try to make a tackle." No sir. It wasn't whether you won or lost or how you played the game, it was merely a matter of keeping your helmet on frontwards and staying alive. Good training for the service, as it turned out.

My biggest asset was also my biggest problem: my brother Jugs. He was All-State and the coaches expected me to fill his shoes when he graduated. At least that's what they expected before they saw me play. After they got a good look at me, they got mad and tried to force me into becoming a footballer, telling me I had to get tough, hit harder, kick butt and take names. But that really wasn't my nature. I was the original "make love, not war" flower child, thirty-years ahead of time. The coaches just didn't understand the limited reason why I was there.

The first game of the season, I hung back on the bench with a gaggle of other ends, hoping that the score would be too close for the coaches to risk putting any of us into the game. Unfortunately, the other team couldn't tackle my brother, and if the coaches hadn't put us in, they would have been accused of trying to run up the score. Remember, this was pre-Lombardi.

I went in and bellyrubbed with the guy across the line from me, being careful not to say or do anything that might make him mad and try harder. He seemed to be after no more than a description himself, and if there was no way we were going to be able to sit this one out, he was likewise willing to dance. This guy had a loud, strained grunt to disguise the fact that he was expending virtually no energy at all. I thought it was such a great touch, I incorporated it into my act as well.

I felt I was doing a pretty good job of blending in, and on defense, even waited to stand up last a time or two after the play so it might look like I had made the tackle. But at that stage of my life, I didn't realize how sharp a coach's eye can be, or that grunts, even great grunts, can't be heard at thirty yards in a crowded stadium. The next practice, I was the center of attention. The center of the bullseye, would be more like it.

The coaches started this particular practice by giving us a talk about football being a team sport; everybody pulling their own weight; how terrible it is to let your teammates down. Then they got personal. Asking me whether I had been in love with the guy blocking me since all I had done for a quarter-and-a-half was slow dance with him, and he was obviously leading me. They said the first part of practice for the linemen, including us odds and ends, was going to be a drill on splitting the double team. I was invited to assume the down position across the line of scrimmage from the rest of the linemen who were divided into two long lines, a yard or so apart, both pointed at me. The fix was definitely on.

The coach blew the whistle and one guy hit me high, the other low. It was like a blast from a double-barrel shotgun. I countered the best way I knew how: by going limp. The coaches saw my lack of gumption and went pretty much berserk. They sent wave after wave at me, two by two. I felt like the guy at the end of Noah's gangplank when the boat finally docked. I barely had time to get to my hands and knees before the next blast knocked me on my back.

On about the fifteenth double-team, two of the bigger boys picked me up and ran twenty yards to midfield with me before finally slamming me down and pouncing on top of me. All of the air I ever had in me and half the juice come squirting out. I remember looking towards where the backs were practicing and wanting to scream for Jugs to come help me, but I didn't have enough air to gasp with, much less to manage an audible scream for help. The coaches were doing the screaming. "Don't be looking for your brother, Jackson! It's time you stepped up yourself and quit trading off his name." That was the point. I *was* trying to make my own name, or at least get a description attached to it. I just didn't know that meant I had to be ready to kill or be killed to get it.

The coaches stood over me and screamed at me to get up. I figured if I was going to die anyway, why die in a three-point stance. So I just curled up in the smallest ball I could make of myself and hoped it would get dark soon.

Well, the coaches decided they would have to teach me a lesson before they killed me, and with me laying on the ground like a squashed armadillo in the middle of the highway, they kept sending these guys raining down on me. Whistle. Boom! Boom! "Get up, Fielder!" Whistle. Boom! Boom! "Get up!" I remember crying and not being embarrassed as much as being glad about it because it meant I had to still be alive.

I thought for a minute I might be dreaming when I felt somebody picking me up by the back of my pants and setting me down on my all-fours. Then I heard Jugs saying so everyone could hear, "Okay, little brother, my turn. Let me show you how to split a double team." I crawled out of the line of fire on my hands and knees and had wiped most of the tear-mud out of my eyes when I heard the whistle and saw my brother white-eye the two linemen unlucky enough to be next in line. The technique he used was much more like Sam Huff than Sammy Baugh.

With the two linemen still on the ground and the coaches looking at one another shrugging their shoulders, Jugs came over and knelt next to me, looked square into my muddy eyeballs and said, "You go home, Jackson. You're a baseballer. This game ain't for you. It's for guys like me too stupid to do anything else. Anybody says anything to you, tell them to come see me."

I decided the description I already had behind my name was the best one I could have. "Jackson Fielder,

Jugs' little brother."

I walked off that football field and never set foot on another until I was assigned the job of assistant football coach at Nathan Bedford Forrest High. It was the only way I could get the head baseball coaching job.

So this season, we won our second game but lost the third. Coach Grote had another run-in with Andy towards the end of the third quarter of that game. And again it wasn't really Andy's fault. The student body knew Andy was a senior and knew he had never been in a game. So at the start of the second half, they began chanting, "We want Andy! We want Andy!" Over and over.

I could see Grote doing a slow burn. He controlled himself pretty good until Andy, I guess encouraged by the fan support, walked up in the middle of an offensive series and asked Coach Grote if he's going in. Coach Grote started foaming at the mouth and said, "No. You're not going in. You're going up. I want you to go sit in the stands. Your friends want you more than I do."

Andy smiled a weak smile, but Coach Grote was dead serious. Andy went and sat in the stands, uniform and all. He couldn't have been more embarrassed. Steel Mill Johnson couldn't have been madder.

I walked into the kitchen after the game and found Dixie and Andy playing "name that saint." The air was so thick with dogma I couldn't breathe. I took my supper, a self-made peanut butter sandwich, out to the garage. Dixie was a religious cook, too.   Partial to burnt offerings.

I don't know what got into me, but I thought to myself, this kid's life makes mine look like Disneyland. I've got to save him or put him out of his misery, one. I made my rescue attempt during a break in the action for Dixie to go find a pencil and some paper so she could diagram the hierarchy of archangels. I motioned for Andy to come out to the garage. He followed me like a hungry basset hound puppy. If he had a tail, it would have been wagging.

I asked him, "Andy, do you really like talking religion with Mrs. Fielder?"

He said yes, he did. And I think he really did, poor kid.

I asked him what it was he liked about Catholicism.

He said he thought the bells.

I thought to myself: This is going to be like taking candy from a baby.

"Andy," I whispered, "have you ever heard of Einsteinism?" He said he hadn't. That was good. He was an honest simpleton.

"It's a great new religion that I belong to. You know who Einstein was, don't you?"

He said he didn't. Maybe there is such a thing as being too honest. Or too simple.

I asked him if he ever heard of the theory of relativity, or physics, or the speed of light, and he got this real puzzled expression on his face. I got all the way to just plain "light" before he acted like he recognized a word I was saying.

"What's so good about this new religion?" he asked me.

I decided to start with something he could understand. "Well for one thing, no church."

"Is that legal?"

I said, "Yeah, it's legal. You don't think old Coach

Fielder would do anything illegal, do you? Why are you squinting like that son?"

He said he was thinking.

Not easily discouraged, I tried to take advantage of this rare act of concentration by telling him about the photographs taken of the stars nearest the sun which confirmed Einstein's *General Theory of Relativity.* I could have been talking Latin. I was losing my first sheep, but I kept herding. We missionaries, we're like that.

During my sermon, something I said, no telling what, must have ricocheted off the inside of his skull and into the bitesized bundle of nerves that functions as his brain, because I saw the squint lift for a moment.

"You got any of those swinging smoke pots?" he asked me.

Maybe there was a chance if I thought fast. I said, "No swinging smoke pots, Andy, but we do use telescopes a lot." I lied.

"Far out!" he said. "For what?"

"To look at heaven."

"Far out! Have you ever seen a guardian angel?"

I told him no.

"Archangel?"

"Sorry, no."

I explained to him that you didn't need a guardian angel if you were an Einsteinic because of Rule Number Two: Nobody hits nobody.

At that, he alternated raising his eyebrows to his hairline and then squinting until I got concerned he might be trying to work his eyeballs out of their sockets. I told him to please quit before he hurt himself.

Then he asked me the sixty-four thousand dollar

question: "Well, what happens if somebody *does* hit somebody? Say I get hit. What's the difference if I'm a Baptist or a Catholic or an Einsteinic?"

I thought for too long trying to come up with an answer for that one. Finally, to be nice, he said: "No thanks, Coach Fielder. My dad won't even let me be a Catholic, and Catholics can hit their kids as much as they want. He'd never go for Einsteinism."

He had me. What *do* you do when somebody hits somebody?

I let him go back inside so he could rejoin the ecclesiastical seminar already in progress. Gale Sayers and I had some serious soul searching to do. I finished my sandwich and drove to the stable to feed my flock.

Coach Grote watched the game films the next day and analyzed our problem as an "unwillingness to stick." He had the same reason for every game we had lost since I started coaching with him. Not surprisingly, he diagnosed the same problem with the Vietnam War from watching the evening news. Maybe he was right.

Coach Grote also had one diagnosis for every injury. No matter how severe, how bloody, how crippling, he'd look at it, roll his eyes and say, "I've had worse on my pecker, son!" I hope somebody has the presence of mind when he dies to carve it on his tombstone.

That week, to cull out the non-rabid on the team, Coach Grote invented a new drill called "stickin' chicken." He split the team in half and each half lined up single-file on the sideline, twenty yards apart, the first guys in each line facing one another. When he blew his whistle, these two guys would run full speed at each other along that line and they were supposed to hit helmets, full speed, at or about the midway point between them. A drill inspired by a locomotive collision.

You'd be surprised at how much speed a high school kid can build up in ten yards and what kind of noise plastic helmets can make when they hit. If anybody slowed down or veered off, Coach Grote was on them. I never saw the man act any crazier than he did that day when we were "stickin' chicken."

About ten minutes into the drill, the kids hiding in the back of the line finally moved up to the front. A boy named Wally Spitz happened to match up with Andy. Wally was about a 120-pound split end with eyeglasses thick enough to see into the future·and with a body you'd sooner see in Moscow dancing on point as on a football field. Andy goes about 240 and literally makes two of Wally Spitz. At first, everybody was laughing at the mismatch, and I told Andy to swap with the next guy in line. Coach Grote wouldn't have none of that. He told Andy and Wally they were going head-to-head, and he'd allow them both the chance to prove once and for all whether they were real men.

All the kids fell out of line to watch the eighteen wheeler hit the deer. Looking back on it, I guess I could have stepped up and stopped it, but at the time it didn't seem any more than the usual, mean-spirited, football sadism that all America has grown to love.

All the attention the two boys were getting had their adrenaline pumping, and they both came out of the blocks like they had been set fire to. They hit square, head to head. As soon as I heard the strange sound, I knew it meant either traction or funeral, one. It wasn't the sweet crunch of colliding plastic helmets, but the sick crack of lightning splitting a dead pine tree. Andy never stopped running. I don't think he even slowed down. Wally fell on the ground and stiffened up like a dead cat, grabbing at the small of his back and screaming like a girl.

I looked over at Coach Grote, and I could tell he knew he had messed up. He blew his whistle and yelled that practice was over and sent some of the boys after his truck. He rushed Wally to the emergency room. No remark this time about having worse on his pecker.

I stayed at school, wondering how bad it was, until everyone had showered and gone home. I remember walking out to the field before I left for the hospital. I don't know why. It just seemed like I was forgetting something. I found one of Wally's cleats on the forty-five yard line. It marked the point of impact. The laces were still tied.

Coach Grote stayed up at the hospital with Wally almost round the clock through the kid's back fusion. The funny thing was that when Wally's father, himself one of the Horse Backers, got to the hospital, the first thing he did after talking to the doctors wasn't to pistol whip Coach Grote but to come tell Coach not to feel bad because he'd done so much for Wally and was largely responsible for turning Wally into a young man. He told him playing football meant more to Wally than anything else in the world.

I knew Wally. He was in my civics class, and he was a good kid. I also knew the only reason Wally had come out for football was because his father wanted him to be the next Joe Namath and had shamed him into it. The only thing Wally and Joe Willie Namath had in common was that they both had ten toes and ten fingers, give or take. And now Wally is a real man. A real man with a real fused back who won't be able to use a wheelbarrow for the rest of his life, much less play pro ball.

10

It seemed like after each loss, Coach Grote got crazier and the team cared less about football. The kids started holding bonfires on Saturday nights after Friday night football games. When the bonfires started, I understood they were going to be more like pep rallies, and I didn't have any problem with my boys going. It turned out, though, they were mainly just an excuse to get a girl on a blanket several miles from the nearest telephone.

Neither bonfires nor pep rallies nor extra wind sprints seemed to help. It got worse. The next game was against Lee High. They weren't even a Quad-A school. They were barely Triple-A. They were the silk-stocking kids whose parents bought them Vettes and Mustangs as rewards for passing their driver's license exam. Coach Grote hated Lee High worse than life itself.

They have one great back. You might have heard of him, a kid named Shaddock. He'll end up playing at a major college somewhere. Mark my words. He ran back the opening kickoff on us, then proceeded to run through us pretty much at will. What's more, we dropped a dozen passes that if we had caught any four of might have kept us in the game. It was embarrassing.

After Shaddock's fourth touchdown of the first half, our kids were starting to give up. Knuck, bless his heart, tried to show some gumption and take charge. He caught Coach Grote by the arm on the sideline, which never has been a good idea even for me, and said, "Let me key on Shaddock, Coach. I'll break him in half." Coach Grote jerked his arm away and, in the same motion, swatted Knuck on top of the helmet with his clipboard. He yelled at the top of his lungs, "Break him in half? You can't even break his stride! Get out of my sight, Dickweed!"

It was hard for me to watch that, especially with it being my son getting hit and yelled at. But such is the life of an assistant football coach, or assistant anything, I guess. Watching the guy in charge and feeling like you could do better.

Although I was officially an assistant football coach, I had been making a lot of the head-coaching decisions for many years. At least I'm pretty sure I had been. I'm not absolutely sure, because ever since I met Coach Grote nineteen years ago, he called all his players by the same name, no matter how well he knew or liked them, whether he was congratulating them or jumping in their shorts. No matter what the occasion, it was always "Dickweed." In a game, I'd be following him up and down the sideline and he'd say to me out of the side of his mouth, "Put Dickweed in at tackle, we gotta plug that hole." Well, I'd have to figure out which tackle he wanted to take out and who to replace him with.

The only time I remember him overriding my decision was when I tried to sneak Andy Johnson into a game. He yelled at Andy as he trotted onto the field, "Come back here, Dickweed! Don't ever run out onto a football field wearing a Nathan Bedford Forrest uniform until you've actually seen me dead in my coffin. And then come ask me."

I don't think Coach Grote hated Andy. You couldn't. He was a good kid. And Coach Grote was a decent man. But I got no doubt that Coach Grote hated Andy's father and that it carried over. Like I say, Steel Mill is the head of the Horse Backers and, in general, the biggest horse's back in town.

After Coach Grote clipboarded him, Knuck went and sat on the end of the bench. Even with his face all taped, I could tell he was pouting. I sat down next to him and tried to put my arm around him. He moved down to the far end of the bench while our offense drove down the field and missed still another pass in the end zone to end the half.

I expected Coach Grote to really blister the kids at half time, but for the first time in all the hundreds of half times I had been with him, he said nothing. Not a word. There was nothing said by anybody for the whole fifteen minutes. The kids didn't know what was up, but they knew they were witnessing history.

About three minutes before the half-time show ended, Coach Grote stood up, walked through the team, out of the locker room and out onto the sidelines without saying nary a word. Me and the team followed him like naughty puppies who had been found down the street after digging out under the fence. He never looked back.

Coach Grote stood all by himself at the fifty-yard line watching the crack Nathan Bedford Forrest High marching band build to their grand finale. I'm sure it was the first time Coach Grote had seen the band perform in thirty-five years, and the fans were watching him instead of the show.

On the final blast from the dozen or so sour trumpets, the head majorette, who was also on the fifty-yard line not ten feet from Coach Grote, slung her flaming baton at least a hundred feet into the sky. As she circled under it, I could see her eyes were darting from the baton to Coach Grote, back to the baton. Him standing that close was enough to blow a lion tamer's concentration, and as the last echoes of the horn blast ricocheted out of the stadium, the baton fell through her fingers and onto the field. She looked up into the stone face of Coach Grote, then busted into tears and ran off towards the stands, trying to hide her face in her shiny cape. Coach Grote, calm as a dead catfish, walked out onto the field and stomped on her baton until the flames went out. You could have heard a worm swallow. The band didn't move. No one on either team moved. Finally, from up in the stands, Steel Mill Johnson stood up and yelled, "Hey, Grote! You teach them baton twirlers how to catch, too?"

At that, Coach Grote, old as he is, spun around and broke towards the stands, trailing smoke like a wounded B-29. He hurdled the players bench before I could pull along side of him, head him off, and get him cooled down. No telling what would have happened had he got into the stands. Steel Mill is a nice-sized boy and ten years younger. And I'm afraid Coach wouldn't have fared too well, ex-Marine or no.

The second half was no better than the first. Coach Grote coached as usual, but everything was different somehow. We were too far in the hole. Bridges had been burned. Prisoners had been taken and executed. War crimes committed. Something had to give.

Saturday morning after that third loss, I got to the locker room about 9:00, as was my usual, to start grading the game film from the night before. Coach Grote was already in his office with the projector going. That was unusual. I knew something was up when I walked in and he never looked away from the screen.

After a couple of minutes of silence he said, still not looking at me, that he'd been coaching for thirty-five years. I knew that. There wasn't any way I couldn't know that. Ten times a day since I met him, he worked the count into our conversation, mixing the "thirty-five" with some cuss words. He said, "Can you imagine, Fielder? Thirty-five blankety-blank seasons; thirty-five blankety-blank sophomore classes; thirty-five blankety-blank opening games; thirty-five blankety-blank first losses of the season; thirty-four blankety-blank excuses for not winning the state championship. I don't have another one left in me."

With the look on his face of a man who had lived his entire life at the end of his rope, he told me he had just been visited by Steel Mill Johnson and a lynch mob of Horse Backers. The "executive committee" had offered a number of strongly worded suggestions, some dealing with the defense we were using, some dealing with players we were using or not using enough. They even suggested some specific plays.

Evidently, Steel Mill Johnson, in addition to demanding playing time for Andy, strongly urged Coach Grote to heed their warning or run the risk of being replaced by "new blood." On top of all that, Coach Grote told me that when he got up that morning to meet the executive committee, the first thing he saw was twenty-seven "For Sale" signs someone had collected from around town and stuck in his front yard the night before. No one ever accused the Horse Backers of being subtle.

Coach Grote added a few new cuss words to his usual description of the Horse Backers in general and Steel Mill Johnson in particular. And then he handed me the control to the projector. He grinned wider than I thought his leather face would allow. Right before my eyes he got twenty years younger. He put both hands on my shoulders, looked me square in the eyes and said, "Tell a Marine what you want and he'll get the job done or die trying. But never, ever, threaten a Marine, especially when he's got enough years in to be eligible for retirement."

"Jax, you're a baseball coach by nature. A good head baseball coach by all accounts. But coaching baseball is the opposite of coaching football. In baseball, when you get behind, you've got to get looser, get smarter. In football when you get behind, you've got to get tougher, meaner. You've got to hurt your opponent worse than he hurts you. You've got to let your muscles and your heart take over. Your mind and reflexes aren't much good. Remember that. Maybe you'll do better than me, young blood."

He grabbed his coffee mug and drank down the last few drops of coffee warmed over from the night before. He looked at the mug like he was trying to remember where he had got it from. For nineteen years, I'd seen him alternate between drinking Pepto Bismol and black coffee out of that mug without ever rinsing it in between. It was so dirty I wouldn't have mixed cement in it if I had to walk on it later.

He walked out of the coach's office and said, "It's all

yours, Fielder. This old skink has grown back all the legs he's going to grow back. Don't let the jock sniffers chafe you."

All he took after thirty-five years and about that many ulcers was his mug.

Monday morning, I was called out of my civics classroom to the principal's office. Steel Mill Johnson and some of the Horse Backers were there with the principal, all waiting for me. They told me Coach Grote had tendered his resignation that morning and would be retiring effective at noon. I was being named the *interim* head football coach until a permanent replacement could be found.

Johnson let it be known that unless the team began to win, "interim" would be as close as I ever would get to a head coaching job. When I reminded him I already had a head coaching job -- baseball -- he laughed and said he meant a *real* head coaching job. Baseball was a game, he said. Football was a sport. I asked him what monkey killing was. He sat up in his chair a little. I know he was weighing the pros and cons of kicking my butt right then and there. But he settled back down and flashed me an only-a-matter-of-time grin.

I was still a little bit in shock about Coach Grote when I walked out of the principal's office. Johnson grabbed me by the arm a little harder than he needed to and let me know out of the corner of his mouth he thought his boy Andy had "potential" and ought to be playing. I told him I'd evaluate things when I got the chance.

When I tried to walk away, he squeezed harder and told me my son Knuck had "potential" too but he lacked one thing. I thanked him for his opinion but wasn't going to give him the satisfaction of giving me his expert opinion as to what that one thing was. I shook him loose and walked away, but he wouldn't let it be. Finally he yelled at me as I walked down the hall, "Your boy just doesn't have the killer instinct." I never turned around but said over my shoulder, "I'm not so sure I want him to, Johnson. I've got to sleep in the same house with him. And I keep bats in the house." I laughed louder than I needed to. And I never looked back.

I think, all in all, I had been a pretty good assistant football coach. I sure had enough experience at it. Nineteen years. I was certainly old enough to be a head coach, and I'd considered being a head football coach since college. It was as far as you could go in Arkansas high school coaching, unless you won a state championship and moved up to the college level.

There was many a daydream where I'd imagined the moment when I'd have my own team and could put in my own offense, my own defense and be the one who gives the pep talk. But once the team was actually mine, all I could think about was what in the world I was going to do. Luckily, we were playing the weakest team in our district the next Friday, and we could walk over them even with my coaching.

Coach Grote had a pregame ritual that was very strict, and I didn't dare change it when I took over. At 3:30 sharp the team would go on the team bus dressed in sports coats and ties to the Picadilly cafeteria and eat a pregame meal paid for by the Horse Backers. Then we went back on the bus to the locker room to get dressed out. From the moment the bus entered the school grounds until we finally got to the stadium a couple of hours later, there was absolutely no talking except by the coaches. None. The only time I ever saw the rule violated, Coach Grote took two kids who got to giggling and locked them in the locker room until the bus got back after the game. The object was total concentration. Total seriousness.

Looking out of the coach's office from the head-coaching chair for the first time, I saw the pregame ritual different. The way the team managers laid out the jerseys and pads; the trophies lined up in the trophy cabinet; the players lining up to get their ankles taped; the way nobody could talk except the chosen few; the way the things said had been said every week for so long they'd long since quit meaning anything. It all made me feel like I was in church. All this was another form of mass. Another religion. It definitely had been Coach Grote's religion for thirty-five years. Maybe football was what I had been looking for to give meaning to my life. "Take no prisoners!" is, I admit, a little more energizing than $E=mc^2$.

Well, for this game, my first game as interim head coach, I followed the old mass. We got dressed out in our uniforms and boarded the bus to travel across town to Memorial Stadium to play 0 and 5 Jubal A. Early High. What's that, a fifteen-minute ride, maybe? There was absolute, drop-dead silence as we got on the bus, and before I gave the go-ahead to the driver, I made sure everyone was sitting in his seat with his gameface on.

We'd just pulled out of the parking lot when a shriek came from the back seat of the bus. I thought we must have run over a child or, at the very least, a stray pig. But it was Andy and he was shouting, "Stop the bus! Oh, Lordy, stop the bus!" The driver slammed on the brakes, and Andy came tumbling up the aisle pleading with me, "Coach, somebody stole my father's car! I parked it right there! He's going to whip my butt! You've got to let me off the bus! He's going to kill me! You know he will!"

I told him to go sit down and shut up and ordered the driver to take off again. I felt bad for him. I knew he was probably right. His father would likely kill him. But I couldn't vary the ritual for one person. That's what religions are all about. Rules is rules. Start making exceptions and all you got is a club. Andy stumbled back to his seat and buried his head between his knees.

About ten seconds later, his head pops up again and he yells out, "Coach, my mistake. I forgot. My brother dropped me off." I didn't even have time to turn around and give him my death ray before everybody on the bus busted out laughing. I stood up and tried to restore silence with my meanest, steely-eyed, John-Wayne look, but I couldn't hold it and I started laughing too. And couldn't stop. Everybody cracked up. If they hadn't been wearing pads, somebody would have gotten hurt with all the slapping each other and rolling in the aisle. Like puppies in the pound.

With all that laughing, somehow the ghost of "Coach Grote Past" left the team, and for the first time I felt like the team was mine. But the flip side of that coin was it would also be my game to win or lose, and as the bus got closer to the stadium, I quit laughing.

Because of the bus ride, I did decide to change my game plan in one respect. We were playing the weakest team in the league, and I was determined to get Andy Johnson into the game. Not because Steel Mill had instructed me to or because Coach Grote had refused to but because Andy was a senior and had been practicing, running wind sprints, and drinking out of mud puddles for three years now and deserved to get his jersey dirty. And maybe even earn a skull and crossbones.

About midway through the third quarter, I got my chance. We were up by four touchdowns and, with great fanfare, I yelled for Andy to go in the game at defensive tackle. The whole sidelines started yelling for him to go in. Then it spread to the stands. I looked around and there he was, the only guy sitting on the bench, and, honest-to-God, he's reading a comic book. Somebody threw a cup of Gator-Aid at him and got his attention.

When he finally realized that he wasn't dreaming and that I was really calling for him to go into the game, he started scrambling. The first thing he did was jam the comic book he was reading down the front of his pants. Then he started fumbling around trying to snap his chin strap. He finally ran over to me and I told him to go in at defensive tackle for Budden. I asked him, "Do you know what to do?"

He thought for a minute and answered, "My best?"

"That's good enough," I said, and swatted him on the behind.

He started out on the field and the bench, along with the whole stands, started cheering for him. He got out on the field only about ten yards when he stopped and came running back to me, reaching up under his shoulder pads like he had gotten into some fire ants. When he got to me, he handed me a transistor radio and an ear plug.

I let him play the rest of the game, and I think he stumbled into a few tackles. Anyone objective who knew a football game from the Pope's parade knew Andy couldn't have played for very many high school teams in the state, much less the Quad-A preseason state champions. But the kids knew he had done his best, and, after the game, the team carried him off the field on their shoulders. I've never seen a kid so proud.

The next afternoon he came over to the house with a shiner. He acted proud of it and said he got it in the game. I'd seen him leave the locker room, and I knew he was lying. I figured up until that game, Steel Mill had been trying his hardest to believe Andy was better than he really was and that his boy just needed to get into a game to prove himself. Once Andy finally got his chance, Steel Mill couldn't blame the coaches anymore and his big plans for his son's pro football career vanished. Andy was his third strike. No season tickets to the Razorbacks' games. No Heisman trophy for the trophy case at the front door. Maybe it would have been better for Andy if I hadn't put him in the game. I don't know.

Since I had a perfect record as an interim head football coach, I decided I'd "do my own thing" as they say. I took down all the Vince Lombardi -- ". . . winning is the only thing" -- posters and had sportsmanship -- "it's not whether you win or lose . . ." -- stuff put up instead. I figured it was not only the right thing to do, but it's what I'd been preaching to my own boys all their lives. Maybe with me being a head football coach, I could somehow work my way back into the boys' lives. Get them to like me again like when they were little. At the very least, I felt it would help the team make it through what was sure to be a pretty pitiful five more weeks of the season.

You know, for the first time in my football coaching career, I actually looked forward to going down to the school on Saturday morning to grade the game film. But before I could get down to the school, I got a call from the hospital. One of our starting offensive linemen had been burned pretty badly in a freak accident at a bonfire and was out for the rest of the season. My first major disciplinary action as interim head football coach was to outlaw bonfires forever. Unfortunately for my boys, like everything else I do, it didn't stick.

11

Luckily, our schedule got a little easier toward the end of the season. Also helpful was that some teams got beat up, and we stayed pretty healthy. I sincerely believe good sportsmanship had something to do with us starting to win. Contrary to popular belief, being a good looser doesn't keep you from winning. Good sportsmanship also seems to help prevent a lot of injuries, although you probably couldn't prove it scientifically.

We were seven and three when we played Stonewall Jackson High. It was our last game of the regular season and unless the moon and stars lined up just right, we were all but mathematically eliminated from the district championship, and that meant eliminated from any chance at the state playoffs, too.

I got an uninvited visit from Steel Mill and his executive committee of slant-browed Horse Backers on the Monday before the game. They let me know that *they*, as deserving parents, wanted very badly to win the district championship and were holding me responsible if we didn't. That was just what I needed. I felt like Vince Lombardi trying to coach the Redskins with Nixon giving him plays that wouldn't work against the School for the

Blind.

If I didn't have enough on my mind, I also got an unexpected visit the same day after practice from a recruiter from University of Alabama. He said he was looking at Mike Ross, our quarterback, which I could well understand. Mike is a fine athlete and could play any one of a half-dozen positions in college. What surprised me was that the recruiter also wanted to talk to Knuck. I never considered Knuck major college material because he's too small and too slow. I figured maybe this guy might be trying to curry favor with me so I'd put a bug in Mike's ear and steer him toward Alabama. But no harm in talking. Or so I thought.

I called Knuck and Mike into my office and introduced everybody. Both boys were excited, but Mike was excited and polite. Knuck was excited and cocky. When the recruiter asked Knuck about his speed, Knuck puffs up and says in that charming, modest way Cassius Clay has, "I play to knock their butts off, not to race 'em." When he was asked about his grades, Knuck said, "It all evens out in the long run. After I stick the other guys a couple of times, they'll be as dumb as me." I'm thinking: Who is this kid? Who raised him? And why?

The recruiter points out what a fine academic school Alabama is. He looks at me and I'm waiting for him to wink but he never does. Then he asks Knuck if he's given any thought about what he'll be taking. Knuck pauses for a minute then says, "I'd like to take our station wagon." I could have died. For Knuck, Alabama might as well be Yale. Problem was, the recruiter tells Knuck he is impressed with his attitude. Can you believe it? "This is the kind of young man Coach Bryant is looking for," he says to me in front of Knuck with the straightest of faces. Great! Just what I need to keep him focused on the game Friday. You know what they say: cockiness is the feeling you get right before you're taught better.

Well, practice went terrible that week. We never had worse. First off, it was cold. No one wanted to throw or catch. No one acted like they wanted to play at all, that I could tell. I caught myself being a lot tougher on the boys, too. I would start yelling at them and hear Coach Grote's voice coming out of my mouth. I actually talked about "sticking" people. I called somebody a dickweed once or twice, and I don't even know what dickweed is. Sportsmanship wasn't mentioned at all. Nor was it especially evident.

Of course, the kids had been playing since the middle of August, almost three months, and when the pressure got worse, it started to take its toll on them. We had a couple of fights break out on the practice field, which isn't that unusual, but we also had a couple in the locker room. That was a bad omen.

On the way to the Stonewall Jackson game, which, like I said, with a lot of luck could conceivably be for the district championship, I had to get the bus driver to stop and pull over on the shoulder because the kids wouldn't be quiet. I knew they were excited, but rules is rules.

On paper, we should have made short work out of Stonewall Jackson. They were smaller, slower, and greener. But we didn't play them on paper. On the field, it turned out to be a heck of a game.

We lost the toss and lined up to kick off. The stands, both sides, were going crazy. The kids were going crazy. I was going crazy. Football was in the air, as they say.

Francis, my boy, gets ready to kick off. The team charges in a line and boom -- he gets off a peach. The ball sails into the end zone, which is pretty good for high school and flat out great for Francis. There's no run back.

Our defense is running out on the field, and somebody notices Francis lying face up on the forty-four-yard line and he's not moving. The trainer and I run out there. He's out cold. When he comes to, he doesn't have a clue what happened. I don't either. Nobody saw nothing. I didn't know if he had a stroke, fell asleep, got hit by a meteor, or what. I told him to go sit down and shake it off. He staggered off the field like a goose in a hail storm.

We recovered a fumble on their first offensive series and punched the ball over a few plays later. Francis wobbled back on to the field to kick the extra point, and just kind of knuckled it through on instinct.

We line up to kick off again. This time I'm watching Francis to make sure he's okay. He gets a pretty fair kick off and hasn't even picked up his head when Stonewall Jackson's big outside linebacker, instead of falling back and forming the wedge with the rest of the team, flies up and cleans Francis' plow again. Pow!

This time everybody in the stands saw it, and anyone listening on the radio or passing by the stadium sure heard it. Francis was down and out again. I scream at the referee who was right there looking at it, and he shrugs and yells back at me, "That's football, Coach."

Well, when we finally got Francis up on his feet and back to November, 1969, third planet from the sun, I tried to explain to him what had happened. He was addled but said he was certain of one thing. He said no matter if he survived or not, whether his head stopped hurting or not, whether we won or lost, he was quitting football for good. He had had enough. He said he was through with this stupid game; that he didn't play to get brain damage. He was bailing out on me. His chinstrap was his ripcord. He was trying to unsnap it but he couldn't find it. Over and over he tried. He looked like an old hound dog scratching behind his ear out of habit. I grabbed his hand and told him not to worry. Leave his helmet on. I had a plan. And I drew it up in the dirt right there on the sideline like Jugs and me did when we were kids.

The next time we scored, we lined up to kick off just like we had before. But I snuck Knuck in on the kickoff team about three men down the line from Francis. While everyone else was running down under the kickoff, Knuck was going to ambush their headhunter before he ambushed Francis. A preemptive strike. An eye for an eye.

Well, it worked just like I had drawed it up. Their headhunter was zeroing in on Francis again and never saw Knuck coming from his blind side. Knuck threw a perfect cross-body block and cut him down like a sickle. Our fans went crazy. Our team went crazy. I went crazy. They had to carry the poor fellow off the field on a stretcher.

I'm thinking maybe Coach Grote had it figured out after all. Maybe I'd sold this violence thing short. Gimme some of that old time religion.

After the next defensive series, Knuck came back to the sidelines all excited. He came running up to me and Francis and we all three hugged for the first time in about ten years. Francis told him, "Thanks, brother, you saved my life." The three of us sat there like crackers around a still, smiling like we had no sense at all. Like we were a family again.

We won the game and Knuck secured his spot in the assassins' hall of fame. When all the shouting and towel popping stopped in the locker room, Knuck stood on the trainer's table and retold the story of his "super stick" for the whole team. He told about running full speed but in his mind it was like he was in slow motion. He said he was going to hit the fellow helmet-to-helmet and see if he could knock him out or, better yet, flat out kill him. But at the last minute he decided to cut the guy down low. Knuck said his helmet and right shoulder caught their headhunter's knee just as he planted and Knuck heard the boy's knee explode right in his helmet ear hole. He likened it to the sound of a broken-bat single. He said it was the greatest moment of his life. Even through all the tape on his face, I could tell he was smiling from ear to ear. Sam Huff had nothing on Knuck no more.

Francis and I looked at each other through the steam of the showers for our usual tenth of a second. Francis knew. I wasn't sure any more but knew I should know better. Knuck, on the other hand, didn't have a clue.

On the bus home, we heard on the radio that the miracle we needed had happened. The teams that had to tie for us to win the district championship had tied. It was an honest-to-God miracle in Little Rock. Not a hoax this time. The Nathan Bedford Forrest Horsemen were going to the Arkansas Quad-A state football playoffs. The kids went hog-wild.

I told the team we had won the district championship because we were tougher, meaner, stuck harder, and kept sticking even when we got tired. I told them we had finally got the killer instinct and there was no stopping us.

I didn't look at Francis. I could tell he was staring a hole through me waiting for me to insert some mention of sportsmanship into the proceedings. I didn't. I couldn't. I was like a caveman with the sound of the mammoth's exploding skull still fresh in his memory. I wanted to savor the kill, too. I deserved it. I was way past due.

When we got back to the school, the Horse Backers, along with the normal parents and assorted girlfriends, were waiting for us like we were doughboys coming back from "over there." Everybody was singing the school fight song. Steel Mill Johnson made a point of giving me an alcohol-induced bear hug and telling me how much this win was going to mean to me losing the "interim" in front of my "head." He also said that it looked like maybe Knuck was finally developing a killer instinct after all. Somehow, when he said it, it didn't sound as good as when I had said just about the same exact thing a few minutes earlier on the bus.

The next morning as I graded the game film, I couldn't help letting the film run ahead to the cross-body block. In slow motion I watched that poor boy's knee bend backwards so that you'd have thought he was going to kick himself in the stomach. I got sick to my own stomach. And me a veteran. First thing Monday, I was going to put an end to this nonsense before one of my boys got hurt.

Monday afternoon before practice, there was a lot of cheering outside my office and I went into the locker room to see what it was all about. The kids evidently felt a skull and crossbones was not adequate recognition for Knuck's permanent crippling of Stonewall Jackson's headhunter.

They presented him with a mushroom cloud decal about twice the size of a regular skull and crossbones for what was thenceforth known as the "Thermonuclear Stick." I've never seen Knuck so happy. I didn't give my planned sportsmanship lecture. There just wasn't a good opportunity.

We had a big pep rally Thursday of last week, probably the best pep rally I've ever seen at Nathan Bedford Forrest High. I thought the top of the gym was going to pop off. After the pep rally, the principal came down to my office and asked me if I'd seen my son during the *Star-Spangled Banner*. I asked him what Knuck had done, but he said the problem wasn't with Knuck. It was with Francis. He said Francis hadn't stood up for the Star-Spangled Banner. I told him it must have been some mistake. He said it wasn't and for me to deal with it. "This is Little Rock, not Berkeley."

I never figured Francis for an anti-war protestor. But something was bothering him and as the father it was up to me to deal with it. I put it on my list of things to do right after visiting Einstein's grave and right before swimming the English Channel. Right then, it seemed like my whole life had maybe been building toward winning the Arkansas Quad-A state championship and that maybe nothing was going to stop me. I didn't need any domestic distractions. This was football.

Last Friday, we traveled to Confederate Memorial High School for the state semi-finals. I tell you, that's the place where the law ought to get involved. Give me a badge and I'll fill your jail with delinquent parents. Those people are certifiably crazy. It's the worst place in the state to go play. Ask anybody. They put the visiting locker room under the home team's stands. On purpose. The Confederate Memorial fans stomp on the grandstand till you can't hear a word that's said in the locker room. We wound up warming up in the end zone next to two units of K-9 police. We all knew this was not going to be a Norman-Rockwell kind of game.

On the sidelines before the kickoff, I got the kids together and told them if there was ever a game where they had to play aggressive, where they had to tee off from the opening kickoff, where they had to stick all night, this was the one. This pep talk, which I gave without the first note by the way, was the greatest pep talk I ever heard or read about. It was better than Coach Grote, beyond Vince Lombardi, probably past Genghis Khan. Custer could have won with this pep talk and a better scout. If I could remember now what I said then, it would be on a poster in every locker room and Quonset hut in the country as well as carved on the side of every ICBM.

The kids were rocking. The stands were rolling. The drums were beating. The night vibrated football. The closest I can describe it to you is the climax of the Tarzan movie right before the pygmies tie the ivory poachers to the crossed trees and make a wish. As the kids busted out of the locker room, to a man they yelled at the top of their lungs: "Take no prisoners!" The ghost of Coach Grote had returned to lead us to thermonuclear victory.

We had to kick off first. We covered the kick pretty well, and I heard a bunch of cheering out on the field. Knuck came running off, people patting him on the back. I couldn't figure out what was going on. At first, I thought we might have recovered a fumble or something. Then I saw a kid from Confederate Memorial down on the field.

Their coaches came running out and didn't waste any time hustling him off on a stretcher.

The referees stopped the game, conferred and then came to the sidelines to talk to both coaches. They said that somebody on one of the teams had lost a screw-on, plastic cleat and that the metal post on the bottom of somebody's shoe apparently punctured this kid's calf and tore about four inches of muscle away from the bone. They were rushing the kid to the hospital to get a sewing machine full of stitches. I turned around and was going to tell everybody to sit down right where they were and check their cleats when I saw Knuck on the bench screwing a cleat on the bottom of his shoe, the kids still patting him on the back. I heard him yell in the general direction of the ambulance leaving the end zone, "I've had worse on my pecker, Dickweed." The kids who were gathered around him howled.

I should have sat him on the bench. Heck, I should have turned him over to the K-9 cops. I didn't do neither. I gave him the benefit of a very small doubt. A father's doubt. The Arkansas Quad-A football championship was on the line. As was my life.

You've never seen a high school game with so much hitting going on. It was a knock-down drag-out. We lost about four or five kids to injuries during the first half. I'm sure Confederate Memorial lost at least that many.

In the fourth quarter, Knuck got kicked in the face and starting bleeding through the tape. Everybody in the stadium saw the Confederate Memorial kid kick him, but the refs were thinking about their own families and getting out of town alive and didn't throw a flag. I pitched a flying fit. This was my kid, not to mention my best defensive player. I followed the referee down the sideline and yelled at him, "That's unsportsmanlike conduct! That's not football!" He shrugged his shoulders and turned his back on me. I yelled at him, "You stink!" Without so much as turning around he reached in his pocket, threw his flag in the air, ran to the ball and stepped off fifteen yards against us. He put his foot on the ball, and before he blew his whistle to start play again, yelled to me, "How do I smell from here, Fielder?"

I took Knuck out of the game at the insistence of the team trainer because he couldn't really tell through the tape how bad Knuck's face was or how much blood he was losing. It was a tough decision for me. Tougher than it should have been.

With the score tied, Confederate Memorial got the ball on their own fifteen with about forty-five seconds left to play in the game. We knew they had to come out throwing, and I decided to take a chance and put in Francis at one of the safeties for his speed. He didn't have to hit anybody, he just had to run and bat the ball down. If somebody happened to catch the ball on him, I told him just to jump on his back and hold the guy around the neck until help came.

Like I expected, they threw a couple of passes under our linebackers and then tried to go for all the money on a fly route down their sideline. Francis played it perfectly. He came back for the ball, intercepted the pass and took off tiptoeing down the far sideline. Nobody touched him for sixty-five yards and he trotted into the end zone. Our whole team had a fit and fell in it, right there in the end zone, wallowing around like red worms in a tackle box. Even our fans started running out on the field, which got the German shepherds to stretching their chains.

I was in the end-zone shoving kids back towards our bench so we wouldn't get a delay-of-game penalty when Francis grabbed my arm. I shoved him out onto the field and told him to go kick the extra point. He stopped and shook his head no.

It was all I could do to keep from clubbing him with my clipboard. I grabbed him by the face mask and screamed into his helmet: "God is my witness, Francis Fielder, if you go soft on me now, I'll kick your butt, so help me!" I punctuated my threat with a slap to the side of his helmet. The expression on his face was as if he had just lost the game. He slowly turned his back to me and took his position on the field. He squibbed the kick, but it turned out we didn't need the point anyway.

They tried a couple of more long passes, but they hadn't done any better than before when time ran out. We win! We're playing for the Arkansas state championship. There is a God and his name is Yahweh.

The kids had just picked me up on their shoulders when a K-9 policeman came over and told me that instead of continuing our celebration, we would be wise to go ahead and board the bus and get a good, fast, running start out of the town. Apparently the rumor running through the Confederate Memorial fans was that their kid had been cut with a straight razor. Enough said. We ran straight from the field onto the bus without taking off our helmets, let alone taking a shower.

There were a couple of police dogs posted at the bus for our protection. The Confederate Memorial fans were quickly turning into a lynch mob and starting to surround the bus, chanting obscenities. They were thicker than red necks at a white sock sale. The police dogs were having trouble keeping them at bay.

As soon as our team bus pulled out of the stadium parking lot, rocks and bottles starting raining in. Glass flew everywhere. It brought back memories of being in a B-29 over Japan. Everybody but our driver, bless his heart, got on the floor. He was so low in his seat I think he was flying by instruments, but he didn't slow down. Nobody got hurt, thank goodness, but it sure took the edge off of winning the game.

On the way home, given everything that had happened, not the least of which was Knuck's premeditated assault with a deadly weapon, I tried to give everybody a little sportsmanship talk, but it went over like the proverbial polluted punch bowl. When you get a talk before the game like what they give you in the service before they ask you to charge the machine-gun nest, when kill-crazy violence is the obvious key to winning, and when grownups cuss and stone you after the game, it doesn't make much sense to hear that it's all just a game and you need to play for the fun of it. Be a good sport? It's not whether you win or lose? And don't forget to keep your helmet on and your head tucked between your knees until the all-clear is sounded.

Before we got back to the school, I made a point to walk to the back of the bus and tell Francis how proud I was of him. His head was stuck down in his shoulder pads so far he looked like the headless horseman. I asked him what was the matter, but he didn't answer. The bus was too noisy for us to talk anyway.

When we got back to the high school, there was twice the crowd there had been the week before. All the girls and half the moms hugged Francis before he could fight his way into the locker room. He was the reluctant hero, like it or not, and I couldn't have been prouder, or, to tell you the truth, more surprised. After forty-seven years, I, my ownself, was slowly but surely turning into an overnight success.

You've never seen a happier bunch of kids in a locker room than these kids. To start the season like they did and make it through the semi-finals, with me as their coach, is one of the greatest feats in Arkansas high school sports history.

Now, I knew full well that part of my job as a coach and a father was to discipline Knuck for what he had done. But I decided I could do that at home on Saturday. My most recent failed attempt at noncorporal discipline had been to threaten to make him get a job after school. He didn't like that idea one bit. I explained that it wasn't too early for him to be out working. I told him that when Abraham Lincoln was his age, he was supporting himself. He told me that when Abraham Lincoln was my age, he was president. I put disciplining him on my list of things to do right after we won the state championship. I thought it could wait.

I had no idea what was coming when Francis came in the coaching office and shut the door. The first thing that ran through my mind was, *Oh, no, not the shower talk again.* But I wish that's all it had been.

He said I needed to call the referees and forfeit the game. When I asked him why, he said that on his touchdown run down the sideline, he had taken three full steps out of bounds. His touchdown should not have counted. He said I had to do something. That it wouldn't be right for us to win the game like that.

I tried to explain to him that that's just part of the game, "That's football," I said. But it would have been easier to explain to somebody who wasn't my own kid and if I hadn't been contradicting everything I had tried to teach him for the last sixteen years.

We argued about it, and he tried to make me promise I wouldn't just let things stand like I usually do. I told him the best I could do would be to check the statistics and since, at worst, we would have tied without his touchdown, I'd see who had the most first downs. Because first downs were used in the playoffs as the tie breaker in tie score situations, chances are we would have won anyway. He didn't wait for me to check the statistics. He said he'd get his own ride home and walked out.

I checked the statistics and they had one more first down than we did. But again, maybe we could have got one or two more before the end of the game. What if? You never know. If your aunt had a moustache, she'd be your uncle. Or the head of the Women-Who-Wish Club.

I was thinking about what to do when Steel Mill Johnson and all the Horse Backers came pouring into the office, smelling like Old Granddad, pumping my hand, slapping me on the back, shoving cigars at me and congratulating me for what was for them no doubt a thrilling, vicarious experience. Even if it *was* part of their second childhood. They told me Tara High, El Dorado, had won the other semi-final game and that we'd be traveling there this coming Friday to play them for the state championship of the great and sovereign State of Arkansas.

It was a surprise even to me when the Horse Backers

told me they were going to pay to charter a Greyhound to El Dorado for the team. As sort of a peace offering, I told Johnson he could announce it to the team. The kids went crazy.

Knuck and I rode home together without Francis. We sang the school fight song. Neither one of us said anything about the missing cleat. Tomorrow, I thought. Tomorrow. Licks. Licks are due and owing. Past due.

Francis had showered at home and was in bed by the time we got there. Knuck wanted to wake him up and congratulate him again. I told Knuck to let him be. Francis was tired and not himself.

I noticed when we got home that I had kept the two-minute warning feeling in the pit of my stomach. It had always gone away shortly after a game. Not this night. I took this as another bad omen.

12

There wasn't a lot of talking around the Fielder incubator on Saturday morning. I went off to school early to grade the game film and, by the time I got home, the boys had gone their separate ways. I had an eerie feeling that something was wrong with the space-time continuum, and maybe that's why I called Little Jackson at his apartment in New York.

He said he was getting ready to go out with some friends to a club to watch Arkansas play on TV. After some forced small talk about how he really pitched this past season compared with how the stats said he pitched, I asked him whether he thought I should whip his little brothers if they really, truly deserved it. He knew his little brothers well enough to know that it was a virtual certainty I was talking about Knuck rather than Francis. He said he didn't know.

I asked him how he felt about having been whipped as a boy. He said he didn't particularly enjoy it, but that he didn't ever remember getting whipped unless he deserved it. I asked him what he thought about me not whipping him. He paused for a few seconds and said, "Jaxdad, I know you didn't whip me because that's what you're all about. I know mom whipped me because that's what she's all about. If you're asking whether I would have rather not been whipped by her or been whipped by you, I don't know. I never knew it any other way. If you're asking which of you I think loved me, I don't know. If you're asking if I loved either of you, I don't know that either, so maybe it didn't make much difference to me."

Then he asked me if I knew why he didn't come home more often. I say I don't. And I didn't. Other than I figured he was still embarrassed for stealing the concession stand money. Same as I would have been.

He tells me it's because I always made him feel like he was adopted. What? I couldn't believe what he was saying. I waited for a second for him to say he was kidding, but he let it stand. He was our only child for seven years. I saved him from his uncle-daddy and raised him as best I knew how. Nobody ever called him "stepson" or "half brother." He never missed a meal or a Disney movie. I taught him everything I know about baseball. I admit I didn't know the best way to raise him particularly -- not because he was adopted, but because I was young and still raising myself. But I did the best I could and I never, *ever* considered him any different than the rest of my kids.

At first, I was just hurt. Then I got kind of aggravated. Was this why he stole the concession stand money? Was this why he had been avoiding the family for the last ten years? Or was this just a convenient excuse for acting like a jerk? I asked him what it was exactly that I did that made his childhood so terrible, to give me an example. He hemmed and hawed for a while, but I pressed him on it. I was mad and getting madder.

He reminded me of the summer when he was eleven and I coached his little league team. He said that I didn't pick him for the Allstar Team even though he was one of the two best players on our team. I told him that I couldn't do anything different. I said, "You weren't that much better than Todd Prudhomme, if any. And if I picked you, it might have looked like I was showing you favoritism." He screams at me from a thousand miles away, "Favoritism! I just wanted to be equal. You always rode my butt harder than anybody. I always got pulled out of a game for making a mistake. I always had to stay after practice to hit an extra bucket of balls. Name one time you ever made any other kid hit balls until his blisters popped. You remember that? Popped! I would have rather had a whipping."

I admitted I did remember, but I explained I just wanted him to have the chance to stick in the majors. Not just play. I played. Playing is nothing. It's sticking.

He said, well, now he was in the majors and he hated it. He hated the people, the traveling, the press, the pressure. Pretty much the same things I hated the weekend I was there.

"So why did you make me play?" he screamed again.

I said, "Because I love the game and I love you."

He said, "It's not a game. It's a poor substitute for life."

There was a long silence. Finally, he said, "If you want my advice on whether you should whip Knuck, I'd tell you no. It ain't in you. Like you used to tell me when I couldn't put the ball over the plate, 'Don't force it.'"

That was about it. I made some awkward joke about

dumb ball players and New York night life. He said to tell everyone hello. I hung up not knowing what I was going to do. But I knew one thing. Something had to be done to reassemble my family. To heck with the Arkansas Quad-A football championship.

Now we finally come to last weekend. I still shake my head hoping I'll wake up and it'll be a bad dream.

At supper Saturday, Knuck informed the family in general that he was going out that night to a hayride at the stables where we keep Gale Sayers. Francis said he was going too, but separately. After a little bit of cross-examination by Dixie, we found out that this so-called "hayride" was pretty much nothing more than an outlawed bonfire without the fire and that Knuck had been the one who arranged the whole thing. The team had gone in together and rented the stables from the old man who had sold us our horse.

Francis was excited because it was his chance to show off to the kids the thing he loved the most, Gale Sayers. Knuck got his chance to just plain show off. I figured that without the fire, chances of somebody getting hurt were slim to none, so I told them they could go. I should have known better.

About 10:30 I was getting ready to turn in when I got a call from Dr. Stark, my vet, telling me there had been an accident, that he had to put down my horse and hoped that was okay. He said he was sorry because he knew how much the horse meant to me. Before that moment, I didn't realize anyone else knew. My eyes watered up for the first time since Rosie died, but I swallowed it down.

I told him I was sure he did whatever he thought was best, I asked him for some details, but he didn't have many. He said the party had broke up and he expected my boys would be home directly. I thanked him for all he had done for us over the years.

I had to wait an hour until Francis finally got home, and I was able to piece together what had happened. In the meantime, I tried to decide where a horse goes when he dies after having been baptized an Einsteinic. We hadn't done too much pondering on death and the hereafter, me and Gale Sayers. Mostly we were trying to figure the here and now.

It turns out that to impress the girls, I guess, Knuck saddled up Gale Sayers for the first time in eight years and started doing some fancy night riding. Probably about as fancy as the first and last time I had rode him. Francis chased Knuck around on foot and threw sticks and dirt clods at him trying to get him to stop, but Knuck wasn't listening. Kids think they're immortal. Unfortunately, though, horses know better.

In the dark, Knuck ran Gale Sayers into a rusty old piece of farm machinery and broke the poor horse up bad. How Knuck didn't get killed in the process, I don't know. Francis got to his horse within thirty seconds of the accident but there was nothing to do. The kids started coming up to see what Francis was crying about. Francis screamed for the kids to get away, and Andy took off for the stable to call the vet.

By the time Andy got back, Gale Sayers had quit thrashing around. Francis had put Gale's head in his lap and was trying to convince his horse everything would be okay if he could just hold out till the vet got there. Every so often, Francis screamed out to no one in particular wanting to know what was keeping Dr. Stark. All the kids stood around at a respectful distance, even Knuck. The girls were boo-hooing too.

When Dr. Stark finally did show, he gave Gale Sayers a quick once-over with his flashlight and without much deliberating reached in his bag, took out a big syringe, filled it up with painless death, and gave the horse a shot in the neck. Gale Sayers died with his head in Francis' lap and, I decided, his spirit turned into light quanta, traveling in all directions away from Little Rock at the speed of light, and will travel through the infinite universe forever and ever. Amen.

The poor horse had barely stopped breathing when Francis, covered with Gale Sayer's blood, went looking to kill Knuck. I saw him tangle with melons, and if his recurring shower dream was any indication of what he was capable of, I'm lucky Andy was there to get in between them.

Andy held them each by the front of the shirt at arm's length until they quit trying to get at one another. Knuck knew he had messed up, and Andy didn't have too much trouble hustling him away to the Johnson house to hide out until his little brother cooled down. But Francis never really did.

When Francis finally got home and told us that Knuck had killed Gale Sayers, the pet I myself had fed every day for eight years, Dixie told him not to feel too bad. She said a horse is a beast of burden and did not have a soul. Francis said, "Maybe that's true, Mamma. Maybe he didn't. Maybe he couldn't talk to me or hug me. But he's a horse." I gave him a silent "Amen." She never looked up from her rosary.

Francis went back to his room and slammed his door

so hard the crucifixes on the walls rattled. I thought about going toe-to-toe with her on her statement that Gale Sayers didn't have a soul, but how can you debate someone who takes as gospel everything that's written in the Bible and just points to the book and says, "Here. I'm right." Why waste good oxygen? I went to my room and slammed the door.

Knuck stayed over at the Johnsons' Saturday night. I myself didn't sleep much, not just because of the death of my soul mate Gale Sayers, but because I knew something had to be done. My family was disintegrating. My chickens were finally coming home to roast. I couldn't shake that two-minute warning feeling. I didn't know exactly what had to happen, but I knew whatever it was, it was my responsibility to get it done. And it had to happen soon. I'd ignored it too long. Football hadn't been the answer.

The next morning, Sunday past, Francis woke me up at six-thirty to ask me what I was going to do about Knuck killing his horse. I told him I'd deal with it. He told me I'd better or else he would. Not even looking up, Dixie said, "A whip for the horse and a rod for the fool's back." Francis and I stared at her until she finally looked up. She added, "Proverbs," like that was the end of that problem. Francis went back to his room and slammed his door even harder than he had the night before.

A little before ten o'clock, Dixie and Francis left for mass in separate cars. Knuck didn't show. I stayed at home and was seriously contemplating abandoning my self-imposed rule about sparing the rod when the phone rang. A voice I didn't quite recognize asked, "Hey, Fielder, what's brown and pink, has four legs and flies?" Trying to place the voice more than solving the riddle, I said I didn't know. He says, "You give up? Your dead horse! When you gonna do something about it?" It was the old man who ran the stables. I could smell his breath through the wires.

First he told me about the mess the kids had made around the stables the night before. All the beer cans and sloe gin bottles he had picked up already that morning. He also told me he'd found my dead horse. He said it looked like the kids had tried to cut him up with a dull hatchet with a notion to barbecue him but lost their nerve or their appetite, one.

I told him I knew about the horse, that he had run into a piece of his equipment and we had him put down. He told me he was going to call the knacker. I asked him what a knacker would do with my horse. He said he would make him into dog food. I begged him not to. He told me I should come tend to it because dead horses don't keep well in sunshine, even in November. And especially after the skin is broke. He said he wouldn't be surprised if something big wasn't already snacking on him. I asked him what it was he suggested I do and he said I could bury the horse where it lay provided I dug down deep enough.

I told him I'd come right over and not to let anything touch the horse, please. The thought of another animal eating on Gale Sayers made my skin crawl. We hadn't rode the range like Roy and Trigger, but we had explored the meaning of the universe to the best of our limited abilities. I was probably a little ahead of him on the IQ scale, but compared to Einstein, there probably wasn't that big of a difference between us.

I parked at the stables and got my shovel out of the

back of the station wagon. The old man came out of the place he called his office and said he was sorry about my *boys'* horse. I told the old man "thanks" and he pointed with his bloody toothpick to where I would find Gale Sayers.

As I walked into the pasture, he asked me if I needed some help. I told him "no thanks." I could have used a little, but for some reason I felt like it was my duty to bury Gale Sayers alone. No infidels. At that moment, I wanted more than anything else just to dig. Dig dirt. I had this urge to dig a nice deep hole with straight edges. The least I owed Gale Sayers was a decent Einsteinic burial.

It was a good half-mile walk from the stables to where Gale Sayers was laying. I came as close to crying as I had since Rosie's funeral when I saw him all broken and sliced up like a toad throwed by a mower. Stupid kids. If it ain't a thrill, don't bother them with it. If it is, it don't matter who gets hurt. Somehow, I think if it had been a dead human being laying there, I wouldn't have felt no worse. At least a man has some choice as to what happens. Not Gale Sayers. He has to run where his head is pointed no matter how stupid the fellow doing the pointing.

I started digging the hole on the other side of the horse's back. I planned to dig a fine square grave, six feet by eight feet by six feet deep and then to use the horse's stiff legs to flip him into it when I was finished. I didn't care how long it took me to do it. I was going to dig the perfect hole for the perfect horse.

That, at least, was my sincerest intention. That is until my back started going out on me. After a good three hours, my hole was long enough but only about three feet wide and three and a half foot deep. And I was burning out fast. I had missed lunch. The N.F.L. game of the week was on. Whatever soul Gale Sayers had once had left the solar system and joined Einstein for sure by now. Here I was spending my hard earned Sunday, the one day a week I had off, trying to make a dead horse proud of me. I decided the hole was deep enough. Gale Sayers would be the first to understand.

My back was starting to seize up and I knew I had only a limited number of strains left in me. With a large part of my remaining energy reserves I muscled up on the horse's legs and walked them up until Gale Sayers' four hooves were pointing straight up. Then I rocked him back and forth until he finally fell in the hole, spine first.

It was clear right then that I had underestimated the horse's height. A good two-and-a-half to three foot of legs were sticking up above ground level. I thought about just camouflaging his legs with some pine branches, but that wouldn't do. Maybe if I dug a couple of channels perpendicular to the hole, I could roll the horse over and his legs would fit down in the channels. It was the least I could do. But my back was burning pretty bad now.

I dug for another hour and had the channel for the front legs three and a half feet deep and pretty much complete. I was about two spadesfull into the channel for the back legs when I jumped on the shovel and hit rock. Granite. It felt like somebody stabbing me in the spine with a hot poker. My back now was burning down into the back of my legs. And I started getting mad. Real mad.

I studied the horse and studied the channels. My aching spine confirmed there was only one solution to this problem. The back legs had to go.

Once I made the decision, I was like a man possessed. First I whacked away at the legs with homerun cuts using my shovel. But those legs were as hard as a lightard knot and there was enough play in the horse that I wasn't doing anything with my shovel but making a mess of his hide. Neither would an axe have worked, had I had one. I was going to need a saw.

I walked bent over all the way back to the stable and asked the old man if I could borrow the rusty hand saw that had been hanging on a nail on the wall of his office at least since he sold me the horse. He asked me what I needed it for. I lied and told him I wanted to make a grave marker. He told me not to be cutting down any of his trees. I told him I was just going to cut some dead branches off a dead tree. He looked at me funny. I started to really get angry and had to try hard to hold my temper. My back was killing me and I wasn't in the mood to explain to this old codger what I was going to do with his rusty old two-dollar saw. Finally, he let me have it, but told me at least three more times not to be cutting on his trees.

I straightened up a little on the walk back to the gravesite, but I wasn't sure how much sawing I was going to be able to do. I had to climb into the grave so I could cut the legs off below ground level. I sawed through the muscle okay but the bone was still wet enough that the saw kept binding up on me. I had cut about halfway through one leg when I gave up all together on the hand saw. It was no use. In frustration, I got a running start and threw a cross-body block on the back legs hoping I could bend or maybe break them, but nothing doing. All I managed was to knock the wind out of myself.

Now I was vein-popping mad. I'd been out there in the sun for five hours, give or take, had probably permanently ruined my spine and still hadn't gotten the horse buried. I duck-walked back to the stable and, with the form of Lou Groza, I kicked open the office door.

"Where's your chain saw?" I yelled at the old man. He almost swallowed his toothpick.

"What are you cutting out there? You ain't cutting down my pine trees are you, son?"

"Look here, pyorrhea puss!" I screamed. "Give me your damned chain saw or I'll hire a bulldozer to level this whole stinking spread including all your precious pine trees. Then I'll burn this scrap heap stable to the manure foundation, so help me God!"

He said, "It's cool. It's cool. The saw's in the saddle room. Help yourself."

I grabbed the chain saw, pointed it at him, and said, "If this thing don't start on the first pull, your ass is grass, Dickweed!"

I don't know what had gotten into me. I never talk like that, much less act like that. It was like I had lost control. Somebody else was in charge. Vince Lombardi or somebody. But I will admit this: it felt good.

I hunch-backed one more time out to the gravesite. I climbed down in the hole and pulled the cord on the chain saw. Power! I closed my eyes and prepared to finish the project. Then I hear the old man behind me yelling above the roar of the chain saw, "Hey! Fielder. What the hell are you doing? Trying to make a shetland pony?"

Well, something snapped. The fire that was burning in my spine consumed me. I revved up the chain saw and took a swing at the old fellow's shins. Luckily, his seventy-plus years had been kind to him, and he was able to jump the rotating blade like Errol Flynn used to jump the swords in the pirate movies. He high-tailed it for the stable.

I scrambled out of the hole and took off right behind him, saw roaring. If my bad back hadn't slowed me, so help me, I would have ended up burying a shetland pony and a seventy-year-old midget. As it was, I cut down a dozen of his pine trees, a hundred yards of' fence posts, clipped Gale Sayers and then buried his saw alongside my horse and his legs.

When I finally got back to the stables, I could hear the old man up in the hayloft screaming something about the police and a straight-jacket, but I ignored him. I didn't even bother to open the gate on the way out, but crashed my car right through it like you see in the movies.

I headed back to the Fielder house to start a new era, an era long overdue. No more Mr. Nice Guy. No prisoners.

I swung my Rambler wagon into my front yard at about forty miles per hour and, with the flick of my wrist, took out the St. Francis of Assisi birdbath. It exploded on impact. It felt good. Great. I noticed, too, my back was now cured. A miracle. Alleluia.

I marched into the garage and grabbed my ancient fire extinguisher. I pulled the pin and test fired off a couple of clouds of CO_2. With the energy and clarity of mind of a saint on an all expense paid mission for God, I kicked open the back door leading into the kitchen and yelled at the top of my lungs, "Church is out! Take no prisoners!"

When I got to the living room, I found Dixie in my recliner in front of the shrine bar, crossing herself, her eyes big as Christmas Eucharists. With one long blast of the fire extinguisher, I blew out every candle in the shrine bar.

I turned the extinguisher on her at point blank range and told her, "Get out of my chair. I'm watching the game of the week. If you don't like it, bundle up your relics and hit the convent, sister."

She could hardly talk. But she managed to stammer, "You're crazy!"

I said, "You're right. I am crazy for letting my family disintegrate before my eyes. For letting you use religion as novocaine. For letting Little Jackson use isolation as novocaine. For letting Knuck use violence as novocaine. For letting Francis waste his life trying to get a fix of mother's love for his novocaine. No more novocaine. We are going to live life even if the pain kills us. Now get your sacred butt out of my chair before this thing goes off."

You know what? She did. Another miracle. She didn't say another word. She slowly looked around the living room like she was taking it all in for the last time and went back to our bedroom with her tail tucked between her legs.

Next, I went back to Francis' room. I kicked the door in and fired a short blast from the extinguisher to make my entrance more dramatic. Francis was sitting at the foot of his bed staring at me with his mouth hanging open.

"You've got one more football game and then, win or lose, you're through with football. You're a baseballer, and it's football that's making you crazy. Violence runs against your nature. That's why you're having those nightmares. And what's more, you're through with church, too. If I ever catch you hanging around a church again, so help me, I'll whip your butt. You understand?"

His mouth never closed. I walked out. I drug my recliner back in front of the TV, sat down with my trusty extinguisher in my lap, and watched the rest of the game of the week. During commercials, I swiveled my chair around and watched Dixie dismantling the shrine bar.

I caught Knuck sneaking back in for some clothes about seven o'clock Sunday evening, and Dixie took first crack at him for missing mass. Knuck always used as his excuse the fact that I don't go to mass every Sunday either. The Monsignor called me his "Seventh-Day Absentist."

I went to mass regularly as long as I could, but in recent years, it's been harder and harder to sit through. Church to me was like the monster that ate my wife and was in the process of eating one of my boys. Dixie acted more hurt than mad that I didn't go. In her saintly manner, she would say as she walked out the door without me, "If I get the keys to heaven, I'll let you in." I always thought to myself, *Why don't you get the keys to the other place and let me out?*

I told Knuck we had to talk. He said we could talk tomorrow at practice. I told him I had news for him, he wasn't going to be at practice. He looked at me puzzled at first, then his stare turned to icy hate. Same hate I had seen on Little Jackson's face the day he left home.

He said, "What are you saying, Jaxdad?"'

I said, "Son, you're not going to El Dorado with the team. You're not playing. Your season is over."

He stuttered, "Why?"

I said, "You know very well why. You want the evidence in writing?"

He said, "Well, that's fine. You can kiss the state championship trophy good-bye. And your job. And if you find another job, you can start saving for my college because I'll never get a scholarship now. Maybe you want me to go to Vietnam and get killed."

Francis had heard the shouting and came in to have it out with Knuck. I told Francis to let me handle it. Dixie decided she'd put an end to this nonsense the only way she knew how and rattled off in her Old Testament voice: "Anyone who reviles or curses his father or mother shall surely be put to death." I looked over at Francis and he was rolling his eyes.

I told Knuck he was grounded until I said different and to go get in his room. He said, "Sorry, Jaxdad, I've got places to be. Things to do. I'm not in training anymore, remember?"

I said, "Son, you're not leaving the house and that's final."

He looked at me like Mat Dillon does at the start of *Gunsmoke* and said, "I'm going to ask you once more, Jaxdad, to move out of my way, please." Dixie screamed out another commandment: "Anyone who strikes his mother or father shall surely be put to death." Dixie, God bless her, will stick to her guns whether they're loaded or not. But, for once, everyone ignored her. Knuck took a step towards the door, and I grabbed him by the arm hard to let him know he was dealing with a veteran of World War II and the American League.

I remember thinking when I grabbed his bicep, *This kid is a rock!* I looked over at Francis and Dixie who were looking at me waiting for the new, improved Jaxdad to handle it. It was either corporal punishment time or it wasn't. I was either going to save my family from disintegration or I wasn't. I balled my free fist up and contemplated just where to best land the first punch. Knuck did the same. I could feel his pulse through his bicep and could hear mine swooshing through my ears. I tried to stifle an involuntary flinch as a painful memory came shooting through my brain filter: the last time I felt one of my kids' pulse -- little Rosie's pulse.

Towards the end, it was hard to get little Rosie to eat. She was vanishing before our eyes, wasting away, getting transparent. But she liked ice cream and she liked to sit next to me on the armrest of my big Chevrolet. So on Sundays and every other day I didn't have some sort of practice, I'd take her to the ice cream parlor for a big cone and we'd cruise around Little Rock looking for all the adventure a dying ten-year-old could handle.

She was usually self-conscious about covering her bald head with her red St. Louis Cardinals cap, except when she went for a ride with me. I guess she figured less chance a kid she knew would see her and point at her like they did every day.

We would roll down all the windows. She'd take off her cap and let the wind whip her two dozen or so ten-inch hairs around her head. She said it made her feel like before she got sick. Back when she had a headful.

One Sunday afternoon, we passed a graveyard and she asked me would I pull in. We had never mentioned the D-word to her and my collar started to get tight on me. I told her it wasn't right to go in a graveyard unless you knew someone buried there. But she acted like it was important to her, so I gave in. She asked me to drive slow so she could read the tombstones. She did the math.

Fifty-six years old. Forty-two years old. I'm sure even the people who died at twenty-five seemed old to her.

We passed a little tombstone with a heart carved in it and she made me back up and stop. She wanted to know why there was no first name, but just "baby girl" somebody or other. I told her it was because the baby likely died before the parents had time to name her. Rosie thought that was the saddest thing in the world, to die without a name. "How could anyone remember you?" she wanted to know. She wanted to know could we name this little girl. I told her I thought it was too late. She wanted to know could we sometime bring flowers to put on the grave. I told her we would the next Sunday and tried to leave.

She wouldn't let me. She said she wanted to get out of the car and go see the little girl's grave up close. I tried to talk her out of it, but it's very hard to say no to a bald-headed ten year-old with big, brown, Bambi eyes. I asked her if she wanted me to carry her, and she said no she wanted to walk her ownself.

She knelt down in the grass and ran her fingers around the heart carved into the marble. She put her cheek against it. She said the cold felt good. After a few minutes she said, "Jaxdad, do you think I could be buried right here next to this little girl? I think we could really be good friends."

I sat down to buy some time. I didn't know what to say or, even if I could think of something, whether I'd be able to spit it out. I had a lump in my throat that took me a long time to choke down. She had asked a serious question and she was waiting for a serious answer.

I dropped back into punt formation. I told her she

was too young to be worried about such things. That she was going to outlive us all. She crawled over to me, knelt up straight, and put both hands on my shoulders like she had seen me do over the years to a hundred boys in football pads when I needed their undivided attention to make a point. She looked into my watery eyes and said, "Jaxdad, I know I'm going to die before too long. I can feel God trying to pull me up to heaven when I'm sleeping. I just don't want you and Mom and the boys to ever forget about me. I'm afraid I'll be all alone somewhere."

I promised we wouldn't forget her and that if this was where she wanted to be buried, by God, I'd make sure of it. She made me swear I would.

I picked her up and hustled her back into the car. I drove faster than usual on my way back home, and she asked me more than once to slow down. I was wrapped up in my own thoughts when she slumped over and cracked her head on my steering wheel. I pulled off the road and held her, waiting for her to come to. She was so light, it was like holding a pillow with a coat hanger in it.

I watched the knot raise up on her forehead and thought about the cancer eating her body. I listened to her soft breathing for what seemed like an hour. I pressed my lips to the lump and I could feel her pulse. I prayed to God to give me the cancer. To transfer it through her bald head, through her clear skin, through my lips into me, and let her live. Let me die.

When she did come to, she said we had better go home. She felt sick. She apologized and said she was having a bad day.

We went for ice cream one more Sunday. We put flowers on the little girl's grave and sat in the grass and both ran our fingers around the heart in the marble. We agreed on a name for the little girl: Wendy? Wendy.

I turned Knuck loose. I just couldn't hit a kid I taught how to tie his shoes. I just couldn't.

He stormed out.

After Knuck left, Dixie piped up and said, "How can he raise his hand against his father? If I had known you were not going to discipline him, I certainly would have."

I said, "Dixie, this ain't about who is raising whose hand. We're losing him. Don't you see that. I may not be able to hold him anymore, but I can't believe hitting him will make him any more likely to stay."

Francis stepped past me and into the doorway, pointed at his mother and said to her, "What do you care, Mamma? You don't love us as much as you do a bunch of dead saints. We're all going to hell. You're the only one going to heaven. Why don't we just say goodbye now and go our separate ways." And he walked out too.

Like a marble carver, Francis knew just where to put the chisel for maximum effect. He caught Dixie square in her petrified heart. If Francis had shot his mother at point blank range with a harpoon, I don't believe it would have hurt her more. Maybe there was something still alive in there.

She turned away from Francis, took three steps and dropped to her knees. It looked to me like she was gonna start praying again and, so help me, I was considering kicking her right in the pew pad. But she slumped down on all fours, and hung her head like a sick horse. I said to myself, *This is it. I'm going to have to put her in the mental hospital or convent or something. She's left planet earth for keeps now.*

I stood there not knowing know what to do. To tell you the truth, I wanted to flee, too. I started just to follow Knuck and Francis out the door when she called for me in a voice I hadn't heard since Rosie was alive. It was a soft voice. A vulnerable voice. A mother's voice.

I knelt down next to her, and she reached up and hugged me for the first time in a long time. She was sobbing so hard, it felt like her chest was going to explode. She kept saying over and over, "God, it hurts so bad. God, it hurts so bad." I knew what hurt. I knew.

On the morning Rosie died, I told Dixie about my promise to her. Dixie said it was a Protestant cemetery and that she wouldn't think of burying Rosie there. I begged. I told her I had sworn to Rosie. She ignored me. And that was the end of it. How would you like to shave with that staring at you every morning?

I try to visit Rosie's grave every Sunday. I'm not big on flowers. I leave her the bottom of my ice cream cone. Sometimes I even ride by Wendy's grave on the way home, just to pass on a word or two from Rosie.

13

When Dixie finally calmed down enough to talk through her crying, she said, "Jax, I can't stand it anymore. You've got to help me. My heart can't break again. The pieces are too small. I've been wrong. I know I have. But when I pray, that's the only time it doesn't hurt. But then my boys do. They're hurting in place of me. I can't have that anymore."

I said, "Look, if I've got to do it, you've got to do it. We've got one kid who doesn't know if he wants to *be* a football player or kill them one by one in the shower. We've got another that's trying to see how much pain he can inflict on everybody else before he stops hurting himself. Little Jackson is hoping if he hates me enough, somehow that will cure all the sores on his life. And you're trying to guide them through their problems with a stick."

She said, "I've been teaching them right from wrong for so long, I don't remember how to be a mother."

I told her, "There's nothing but one rule to remember, Dixie. It ain't complicated. Just put your arms around them and don't let them go until the lightning strikes." I had just come up with the fourth rule of Einsteinism.

We sat there on the couch holding hands waiting for the boys to come home so we could make a new start at trying to regenerate a family. My back started hurting again, as did my big toe from kicking in too many doors in one day, but this wasn't the appropriate time to complain. I wanted just to savor the moment.

Francis came back first about ten o'clock. Dixie surprised him by meeting him at the back door and throwing her arms around him. Francis said he was sorry for what he had said, and she did the same. They hugged and cried until I started thinking maybe I had one wall propped up.

The next step in my home rebuilding program was finding Knuck and getting him back. I asked Francis to please go find Knuck and bring him home. I figured Francis would know better where to find him and that Knuck would be more likely to get in the car with Francis than with me. But I was worried that Francis still had a score to settle with Knuck because of Knuck killing his horse, and for a thousand other things over the past sixteen years.

"But he killed Gale Sayers!" he said. Then he looked at his new and improved Mamma and couldn't do anything but. He grabbed my keys and walked out. The last thing he said was, "I'll bring him back, Jaxdad, dead or alive." Let me tell you, that didn't exactly put my mind at ease.

Dixie and I didn't say a word until we finally heard the car pull up into the driveway. It was the longest stretch I had seen Dixie go without saying the rosary since before Rosie died. Out of habit, though her lips and fingers were moving just the same as though she was holding the beads.

But instead of the door opening, there was a knock. A solid, serious, stranger's knock. I opened the door, and a policeman was standing there looking down at his feet. I immediately took this as a bad omen.

The first thing that flashed through my mind was that the old stable man had climbed down out of the hayloft and called the cops on me. But the policeman looked too concerned for a few felled pine trees and a buried chain saw. Or even a dissected horse. When I invited the policeman in, he mumbled "no thanks," still not looking at us. My stomach did a flip. Dixie walked over and grabbed her rosary and started fingering it. She never looked at the policeman again.

The policeman said there had been a serious accident, and he needed me to come with him downtown. I asked him who was hurt, and he said one of my sons. He didn't know which one. I asked where my son was, and he said he didn't know where the ambulance would take him but he would find out. He said the other one was okay. He said he didn't know any more than that.

I figured either Francis had taken this occasion to run Knuck down from behind or that Knuck had beat Francis to a pulp and stolen my station wagon on the way to enlist in the Green Berets. Either way it was not good news.

I rode with the policeman, not downtown, but straight to the hospital. The whole time I'm thinking whether it would be better for one son or the other to be hurt. Knuck was tough as white leather and would recover faster, but if an injury were to mess up his body permanently, I don't know what else he'd have to live for. Or with. Francis, on the other hand, was in a lot of ways stronger and tougher than Knuck, but physically he was puny and less likely to bounce back from a serious injury.

I pined over it like it mattered what I thought; like what I was thinking was somehow going to affect which one had got hurt. Like I was somehow in control of the universe. I wasn't even in control of my own miserable excuse for a life.

We walked into the emergency room, and one of the young doctors grabbed me by the arm and pulled me over to one side. He said he was sorry, but my son had suffered a massive head trauma and they had done everything they could, but they couldn't save him. I didn't hear anything after that. I could see his lips moving but nothing was registering. I just sat down on the floor.

What had gone wrong with the universe that something like this would happen on a cool, fall night in the middle of the United States of America, in the middle of the Arkansas state football playoffs? Why didn't children just grow up like they're supposed to? It ain't hard. All they've really got to do is stay alive. The rest is child's play.

I couldn't help but think of a Japanese woman I saw during the war sitting in the middle of a crossroads holding a little dead girl. She kept calling for me to come help her. Come help her. I thought that was the most pitiful thing I ever saw. But that was a half world away in the middle of a world war. This was Little Rock, Arkansas, nineteen sixty-nine. And nobody could help me, either.

The doctor let me sit a minute, then went and got the policeman again. They both gave me a hand up and talked to me about me identifying the body. They told me I *had* to. I must. I told them to go to hell. They told me it was the law. I told them it wasn't my law and they could quit wasting their breath. I was going home and start the weekend over again. The doctor insisted that if I didn't identify the body, they'd go get my wife and bring her to the emergency room to do it.

There they had me. It had taken me eight years to get Dixie back home. I couldn't let her go again. I needed her. That meant I was going to have to find out which of my sons I'd never talk to again. Which one I'd never hug again.

They took me to a screened-off bed in the emergency ward and told me I was welcome to go spend some time with him. I walked in, and the first thing my eyes hit was one foot sticking out from under the sheet with only a sock on it. On the other foot was an already worn-out Adidas tennis shoe that Knuck just had to have to start school this fall.

It's funny what goes through your mind as you finally lose your grip on the side of the septic tank and your head goes under. I thought about all the tennis shoes he had worn-out in eighteen years and that I had kept track of my boys growing up by their shoes. I was the one bought their shoes. Their mother did all the other shopping, but I bought their shoes. I always hated to throw away the old, worn-out pairs. I don't know why. It was like if I kept them, someday I'd figure out a way to roll back their mileage and they'd be kids again. We could start over. I wish now I had saved every single pair. For me, their shoes would tell more about their lives than an album full of posed photos. Now, I was looking at half of the last pair of shoes I'd ever buy for Knuck.

Thank God I didn't punch him. But I *had* waited just a little too long to hug him. I had blown my chance. I've had three boys, and, somehow, I always failed to put my arms around each one and absorb his pain when he needed it most. Why is it so much easier with daughters?

I stayed there with Knuck for probably ten minutes. It seemed longer. I never lifted the sheet from his face. I couldn't.

I turned to leave and almost ran up on Dixie standing there in the doorway. I hugged her as hard as I could and tried to steer her out of the little cubicle, but she stiffened on me. She said she wanted to see her son, to see her second dead child. Me, I couldn't. I'm sorry, but I couldn't.

I waited for her on the other side of the curtain for what seemed like an hour. I listened but she made no sound that I could hear. The young doctor came back and said the police needed to examine the body. I grabbed hold of Dixie and led her away by the arm. Her face had no expression. None.

The lady next door had driven Dixie to the hospital and was waiting for us in the emergency ward lobby. She put her arms around Dixie and led us out to her car. Nobody talked on the way home until Dixie asked the lady to please take her to the cathedral. "No!" I screamed. "Please Dixie, don't. Come home with me. Francis will need us. Don't run off to church."

The neighbor lady turned around and gave me a dirty look like I had just asked to be dropped off at the pool hall. She said to Dixie, "Don't worry, honey. If church is where you need to be, church is where I'm taking you. There's comfort in the Lord."

I wasn't invited, but got out with Dixie at the cathedral anyway. I followed her around back and watched her find a hidden key and unlock the big back door. As I walked in, I made the mistake of looking up at the tortured Jesus. In candle light He was even scarier than in the daytime. I picked out the nearest stained-glass window and decided that at the first strange noise, I was going out, head-first. I kept my head down and my eyes closed hoping I'd wake up and this night would be just another one of my church dreams. But this wasn't Sunday mass and I wasn't sleeping.

Dixie went straight to the first pew, her pew, and side-stepped down to the middle. She knelt down and started praying her rosary. I gave Dixie her space. I knew she and God had dealing to do. She was either coming home to what was left of her family or she was leaving us for a better world.

I sat a couple of pews behind her and went through the three rules of Einsteinism, over and over. They were no help. Maybe Moses was right to have ten rules. Maybe I had streamlined my religion too much. I asked myself what Einstein would have done in my spot. Emptiness equals man times the speed of his life squared.

After an hour of soul searching, I was about to give up when I remembered the newest rule of Einsteinism, the fourth. According to my religion, all I had to do was put my arms around her, and bring her back to the house. The house was bound to turn back into a home. I was still the head of my family, by God, and a family belongs in a home. Why should my religion take a back pew to hers?

I walked around to the front aisle and stood in front of her. In the toughest whisper I could muster, I said,

"Come on, Dixie. We're going home." I grabbed her hand and tried to pull her up off her knees so I could get my arms around her. She leaned away from me, half kneeling, half sitting. She squeezed my hand hard like she loved me, but the rosary beads hurt as they bit into my fingers. My eyes filled with tears, and in the candlelight, Dixie shimmered like she had a halo. I've never seen her more beautiful. But this time my watery eyes couldn't melt what was left of her heart. In a faraway voice, she said, "Go on, Jackson. Go take care of the boys."

Then Dixie shook her hand loose. All I had to show for forty-plus years of loving her was an empty hand with a wedding ring on one finger, and rosary-bead dents on the others.

I walked home. When I got to my house, the front door was wide open, and it was cold and dark inside. The only light was from the candles at the hastily reconstructed shrine bar. No one was home. There was no more life left in the house. I sat down in my recliner and turned on the TV.

I watched the late night coverage of the Apollo 12 moon shot. They said they shot the rocket off at a certain time, with a certain amount of fuel, and it's calculated *so* exactly that the rocket lands a couple of days later on a spot on the moon that they were aiming at. The rocket's got no steering wheel or brakes. It's like a bullet; its path is set the moment you pull the trigger. It's the same with life. But I feel like someone messed up the calculations prior to my launch and I've been tumbling out of control ever since. No steering wheel. No brakes but bad breaks. And I'm just about to burn up on reentry. Where's Einstein when you need him?

Sitting all alone in my cold, dark incubator, I came pretty close to understanding how those astronauts must feel, separated from all they love, heading, they hope, for their spot on the moon. The only difference between us is there are three of them in the same boat. I wished I had a couple of buddies along on my trip. My boys would work just fine.

Dixie stayed at the cathedral. Her trip back to planet earth had been only momentary and she had decided heaven was better. I'm sure she's right. It says so in The Good Book.

Meanwhile, I went over to my other neighbor's house and had to dodge forty-thousand questions trying to borrow his Maverick from him. He's the one with the bomb shelter left over from the Cuban Missile Crisis. It would have been less trouble to have just walked to the police station, but my back and big toe were killing me.

When I finally got there, the desk sergeant told me Francis was being charged with attempted murder. Up until that moment, I had thought they had been in a wreck.

I had to talk to Francis through a piece of wire-reinforced glass. He sat there crying like he did the day Rosie died. And, really, what had changed in the last eleven years? His eyeballs and tear ducts may have gotten a little bigger, but they were the same eyeballs and same tear ducts. His heart had beat a few million more times, but it was the same heart. And it was broke. I knew if I could just somehow put my arms around him, I could keep him alive long enough for his heart to mend. But the way it was, all I could do was talk to him. Talk. If humans had never learned how to talk, we'd all be a lot closer.

We'd have to touch. And feel. Wire-reinforced glass would never have been invented.

He was crying so hard, I could hardly understand what he was trying to tell me, but eventually I did make out what had happened. Turns out Francis had found Knuck sitting with Andy and the other Johnson brothers in the Johnsons' front yard on one of the several Johnson monuments-to-rust permanently up on blocks. Francis pulled up in front of the house and told Knuck I said he had to come home. Knuck told him to drop dead, and one of the Johnson brothers piped up and told Francis to get lost.

The oldest Johnson brother, the one who was a grade or two behind Little Jackson, that would have made him twenty-six or twenty-seven, for God's sake, called Francis a fairy. Well, Knuck didn't like this remark so he hauled off and cold-cocked the oldest Johnson brother and started wrestling on the ground with the middle one. In two seconds, Knuck was sitting on the middle brother's chest, pounding him in the face. Andy was yelling for Knuck to stop, and Francis got out of the station wagon and started trying to pull him off.

Francis told me exactly what happened next and I believe him. I don't ever remember him lying in his whole life. He said, between big sobs, "Then Mr. Johnson kicked the front door open and came running towards us all hunched over with a crazy look on his face, bootlegging something shiny. He was screaming something about his home being his castle. I could see he was carrying this shiny thing, but I couldn't make out exactly what it was. It was too shiny to be a gun. I was thinking maybe a knife. But it was odd-shaped. It was one of his old marble-based, football trophies. He ran up right behind Knuck and, without as much as a pause, took a homerun swing at Knuck's head with it. Jaxdad, remember how we loved to watch the *Three Stooges* on TV and how Moe would hit Curly with a shovel or a pickaxe and it would make a clanging sound. The three of them would look down and the tool would be all bent? I thought about grabbing it before he swung. I was close enough I could have. It was all in slow motion. But I didn't. I didn't, Jaxdad. And it didn't clang like the Three Stooges. Instead there was the sound of the Virgin Mary hitting the linoleum."

Francis said Knuck made a little noise like White Rose made when she had got jumped by the cat. Then he rolled off of the Johnson boy with his eyes froze open.

Francis, with the bottled-up energy of sixteen years of whippings, jumped on Mr. Johnson like a mistreated spider monkey and, from what I've learned since, gouged out one of Steel Mill's eyes with his thumb before Andy and the other Johnson brother were able to pull him off. They pinned him down until the police got there.

Knuck never moved again.

With his one phone call, Francis had called home and got Dixie. He tried to tell her what happened. She reminded him that the Bible says to bless those who curse you.

Me or you would have taken that as unwelcomed moralizing, but to Francis, that was his mother blaming him for his brother's death. To a kid who had been trying to finagle his mother's love for sixteen years by living like a saint, it was a crucifix through the heart. But you can't fill a hole in a kid's heart with saints and ceremonies any more than you can show him a hamburger commercial and fill a hole in his belly. You've got to hand-feed them.

Francis asked me if I hated him, too. I didn't expect that. I told him through the glass the best I could, "Son, look me in the eyes and listen to what I'm going to tell you. I mean this more than anything I ever told anybody in my forty-seven years. I changed your diaper when a weaker man would have broke and run. I've sucked snot out of your little nose with an awl so you could breathe through the night. I ate a cookie you'd gummed all day just because it was a present from you. I held you all night in my arms when you had the croup, and I was afraid if I put you down you were going to quit breathing. I would have gladly died for Knuck if it was a choice between us. I would trade places with you if I could. If you think I could ever stop loving you, for any reason, your fault or not, then you just don't understand what it is to be a father. It ain't even something I've got to think twice about. I'll get you out of here. I swear."

The last thing he asked me was whether I had seen Knuck. I said I had. He asked me if somebody had closed his eyes. I didn't know but I lied and said yes, somebody had. He said, "Thank God" because he couldn't stand it if Knuck was buried with his eyes open. I told him not to worry.

I didn't see Dixie until nine o'clock the next morning. Monday. Yesterday. She had spent all Sunday night at church and then got in the six o'clock and seven-thirty a.m. masses. A doubleheader. After her second mass of the morning, she paid a visit to the Johnson house to tell Mr. Johnson and the boys she forgave them. They said thanks, they'd try to send over one of Andy's hamburger casseroles.

14

I went to the funeral home on Monday afternoon. I wanted to get there ahead of the Women-Who-Wish Club, which was congregating at my house, making noises like they were fixing to take over the arrangements. When I buried my father thirty years before, I was just a kid and didn't have any idea what I was doing. I wouldn't be surprised if my old Pa wasn't haunting me yet for the send-off I gave him. Then I played pro baseball, went to war, spent time in a prison camp, and half-way raised a family. But when I tried to make arrangements for little Rosie, I was just as useless. Given another ten years and plenty more miles, you'd think I would have got the hang of it. But I hadn't.

The funeral director looked like he was in black and white rather than color. He took my hand to shake it and wouldn't let go. He said he didn't consider himself a funeral director but liked to be called a southern planter. He laughed and said it was a little joke to break the ice. I wrestled my hand away and wiped it off as good as I could on the back of my pants.

The thought of burying my kids and their skin drying up and withering away in a metal box in the ground makes me want to burn down the world. I told the funeral director whatever he thought best was fine with me. I just wanted to get out of there. He did guarantee me Knuck's eyes would be closed. He said they glued them shut. Thanks for telling me.

Driving home from the funeral parlor the strangest feeling came over me. It was a peaceful feeling but at the same time violent and exciting, if that makes any sense. Like watching a house burn down. I didn't know what it all meant until I pulled into my driveway and saw it there on my roof, Rosie's silver stuffed monkey spread-eagle on the shingles above my front door. I was confused. How did Mister Mugs get from Johnson's roof to mine? Then it hit me. I knew. I understood my place in the universe.

There was one thing I had to do before I could bury Knuck. A small thing, but it now made perfect sense to me. I hadn't been born to pitch in the majors, or to raise a family, or to win the Quad-A Arkansas State football championship. I had been born to kill Steel Mill Johnson. For Knuck, for Francis, for Dixie, for Andy. For Son of Ray Bob. For the Black Widowmaker. There were plenty of reasons. Better reasons than I had to kill Japs.

It wasn't that I was especially angry. In fact, once I had realized it was my destiny to kill him, I felt better than I had since Gale Sayers died Saturday night last. The two-minute warning feeling finally disappeared. My life wasn't my fault. It had been predetermined. Finally, a religion I could understand and believe in. Take no prisoners!

With my stomach finally settled, I realized how hungry I was. I couldn't remember when I had eaten last. I felt like donuts for supper. I drove to the donut shop and had one of each kind. Then to Baskin & Robbins for a giant cone. I dropped the tip off for Rosie. I told her her little brother Knuck would be there the next day to keep her company. I hinted I might not be too far behind.

When I got home, I found myself drawn to Knuck's room like bugs to a fat lady's perfume. It was too quiet. No radio. No weights clanging. For some reason, I opened the door to his closet and there were his Converse hightops. I remembered when we bought them. I put them on, taking my time and lacing them carefully so there were no twists in the laces. They fit good. I felt fast. In the corner, back behind five pairs of wadded blue jeans and a sweatshirt that said "Blow Your Mind," was a baseball bat.

When he quit the team this summer, to hurt my feelings, Knuck had made a big show of throwing away all his baseball stuff. I was surprised to see he had saved a bat. But he hadn't. It wasn't his. It had dried blood on it. I recognized it as Andy's 34-inch, Yogi Berra model, monkey-knocking, Louisville Slugger which Knuck must have hid for Andy just in case Steel Mill had any ideas about working his way up the evolutionary ladder. Now I had a chance to do the neighborly thing and return the bat. Show him how much I appreciated the hamburger casserole.

I held the bat in my hands. There's something about a bat. It felt good. It felt cave-man good. I was going to use a bat like God meant for it to be used. Like Cain or Abel, one, used it. Bring on the Hittites. Hey batter, batter.

I got my St. Louis Browns warm-up jacket down from the attic. A little tight, but not so tight that I couldn't take a homerun cut at Steel Mill's ugly head.

I walked outside into late November and took a deep breath. Cool fresh air mixed with the smell of moth balls from my jacket. It was the smell of seasons gone by, of trampled dreams. But trampled dreams was all I had, trampled dreams and a bat.

It was getting dark. The street lights were coming on. It was time. I was due. Past due. Even Einstein, after the war when the Japs got on him about encouraging the development of the A-bomb, he said, "Well, they were after me and my people." Amen, Albert. Amen.

I walked down the sidewalk towards the Johnsons'. With every step I felt younger, freer. After I popped Johnson's head, my problems would be over. No more wife. No more state championship game. No more Horse Backers. No more living a life that hasn't meant nothing for longer than I could remember. For the rest of my life, however short, I was going to live it like it's meant to be lived. I was going down swinging.

There were lights on in the Johnson house when I got there. The bat made a swooshing noise as I took a practice cut. As I came up the walk to the front door past the deceased cars, I could hear Steel Mill in the house yelling at his boys to bring him something. *I* had him something. This was going to be great. Not a practical joke. A knock-knock joke. I swung the punch line again.

As I lifted my foot to climb the first porch step, I heard a sound that froze me cold. It was a sound you never forget, like bullets going through your plane or a crowd booing you. It was the sound of a metal chain being dragged across roots. But how could it be? I looked towards the oak tree and there he was. Back. Recaptured. The Black Widowmaker.

I cocked my bat and he pulled up short, teeth shining in the streetlight. I stared into his black eyes for what seemed like light years. He stared right back into my soul, grinning. I knew that grin from my childhood.

I might have been fooling myself thinking I was soulmates with Gale Sayers. Maybe I was really soulmates with this dog from the gates of hell. Maybe I was a footballer deep inside. Maybe after we taste violence, we all are footballers.

The only difference between me and the Black Widowmaker was that I wasn't chained yet. But I was about to chain myself. And I was about to break another sworn promise to one of my kids. I can't do that.

Slowly, I lowered my bat. At that, the Black Widowmaker stopped grinning. He turned away and walked back into his web, dragging his chain behind him. He laid down on the roots and started chewing on something white. I focused. It was Knuck's missing tennis shoe.

I laid my bat on the porch next to the antenna and took the long way home.

That was yesterday.

Today was the funeral. It was like a dream, too. Or a nightmare. Of course, thanks to our ever vigilant District Attorney, Francis wasn't there to anchor me or help his poor mother.

Dixie was there, at least her body was, in a black dress, a black veil and a black hat. Her spirit has joined the Lord. The few times she said anything to me, her voice sounded far away.

The Women-Who-Wish Club showed up in force, armed with their missals and rosaries. Freshly shaven. Mr.

Bodin, the science teacher, stopped me to tell me he had never been more shocked.

Little Jackson flew in from New York. He hadn't forgotten to pack the chip on his shoulder. He ignored me from the time his plane landed.

The school let the whole senior class out so they could attend the funeral mass. High mass. The school's crack marching band turned out in full uniform and favored us with their stirring rendition of *Amazing Grace* and a slow version of the school's fight song.

The team captain, Mike Ross, eulogized Knuck. He talked about crossing over the goal line of life and Jesus being the quarterback in the real game. He said something about being sure that Knuck had "stuck the Pearly Gates and busted on into heaven." I hadn't seen girls cry like that since the Beatles were on *The Ed Sullivan Show*. He got a kneeling ovation. Too much, too late.

Coach Grote waved at me from the back of the church. He had started letting his crew cut grow out. He looked like Pogo. Skink Grote was regenerating his life. Maybe World War II was finally over.

The Johnsons sent a big flower arrangement to the funeral home. It probably set Steel Mill back several hundred pounds of scrap iron. I saw Andy at the funeral crying like a baby. He had a busted lip. He tried to talk to Dixie but she didn't hear him, I guess. Leastways, she never looked at him.

We buried Knuck next to Little Rosie. She finally got the company she wanted. I hope it hadn't been too lonely for her, or for him. We'd all been too lonely since she left us.

Like I told you, right after we put Knuck in the

ground, I mean right after, several Horse Backers came up to me on the pretext of saying that the players had voted to dedicate the rest of the season and the state championship to Knuck. What they really wanted to know was when we'd be practicing again. They were worried the team was going to lose its fine-honed edge.

I shed the Horse Backers and was about to get back in the limousine with my ex-son and the shell that once housed my wife when I saw Coach Grote standing there off to one side, shuffling his feet and looking at me like he had something he needed to say. I was grateful he had made the trip out to the cemetery. He wasn't somebody you'd ever mistake for sentimental. And I'm sure he didn't want to be there any more than me. I walked over to him and asked him if he had any advice for me, thinking with the big game only a few days away he might be lonesome for the sidelines. After all, it was as much his team as mine. Maybe more.

He put his giant hand on my shoulder, and looking through my eyes into the back of my brain, said one word: "Run!"

I nodded and started to say something about the problem with trying to run against Tara's big defensive line. But before I got it out, his face turned scared almost and he shook me saying, "Fielder, let me try to say this so your baseball brain can understand. Two outs, run on anything! Comprende?"

You ever have the feeling this is the second time you've done the exact same thing? I don't know. Maybe I burned out something watching game films over and over. But I didn't follow what he was trying to tell me. I chalked it up to us both being uncomfortable there in the cemetery. I thanked him for coming. He shook his head and walked away.

When we got back to the house, Little Jackson came back to my bedroom and said he needed to say something to me. To get something off his chest. I told him to come sit next to me on the bed, but he said no thanks, he'd rather stand. For a minute, I thought he was going to tell me everything was okay and that he was sorry he'd been trying to break my heart for the last ten years. Boy, was I wrong. As usual.

He said he was quitting baseball and was going to live on a ranch in Canada. It was not just a ranch, but a "commune," he said, like that would hurt worse. He said he was not going to try to live my ruined life for me anymore. He was going to live his own life. I looked him in the eye. His heart was as cold as his mother's. There was no hope. No hope at all.

Just when I was ready to curl up in a ball until someone blew a whistle to stop the double-team, my brother Jugs came to the rescue, again. I remembered something he had told me the very last time he wrote me. It was at the start of the war. I was still training to be a pilot and he had just seen his first action against the Jap zeroes. I know he was worried about me, what with me being a born baseballer, that I might not have what it takes to go head up with a Jap double team. He wrote: "Remember Jax, there's only one hope for the hopeless and that's to have no hope." I washed out of flight school after he got killed and never understood his advice. I had forgotten it until just that minute. What he was saying was that there's only one way to beat certain death, and that is to quit hoping that you're gonna make it out alive, because chances are you're dead anyway. Just go for broke. You've got nothing to lose.

Here Jugs was helping me twenty-five years later. At forty-seven, I was still Jax Fielder, Jugs' little brother. And still proud of it.

I got up off the bed slowly and reached past Little Jackson, shut the door and locked it. I looked down at his crotch and told him his fly was open. He glanced down. Then, sore back and all, with the technique Dick Butkus wished he had, I tackled little Jackson onto the bed, my shoulder in his stomach, my arms locked around his waist. But I underestimated both his strength and his hatred. He started cussing me like I've never been cussed in English and punching and kicking me as hard as he could in the most effective places he could. I didn't say a word. I just held on around his waist.

He rolled us off the bed and right onto my head. I started to black out but the sounds of Dixie banging on the door trying to get in brought me around. I held on.

He worked his way up on his feet, lifting me with him, still punching and screaming. About two minutes into the round, I felt for sure I had permanent kidney damage and possibly a broken rib or two. Every time I breathed, it felt like an ice pick in my lung. I started wondering whether Little Jackson had somehow got hold of an ice pick sure enough. My back was long gone. But I held on.

Along about this time, I happened to look up into Dixie's vanity mirror. With my focus fading in and out, I recognized my face sticking out from under his arm, red as blood blister, and saw Little Jackson's back, his arms and legs flailing away at me. He bent over and I felt him grab me around my waist and squeeze every puff of air out of me as my feet come up off the floor. Then I saw the reflection of my face getting bigger and bigger until I felt my nose hit the mirror and felt the broken glass slice into my forehead. It didn't take long for hot blood to pour down the back of his suit coat and onto my locked arms.

Little Jackson then went to spinning like the real Gale Sayers, but I held on. I learned on *Bonanza* that the way you break a horse is to stay on him until he figures you ain't budging and trying to throw you is just a waste of good hay. I don't know whether Little Jackson reached that conclusion before or after he saw all the blood, but he finally stopped his bucking. He started calling for his mamma, telling her to call the doctor. Then he started pleading with me to let go before I bled to death. I didn't say anything. I just held on.

Then I started sensing a new movement in his belly - - first it was barely feelable -- a quivering. But it got stronger and stronger. Then I heard him. He was crying. I felt him go all limp. I let go. I had broke him. Me and his father Jugs. And the fourth rule of Einsteinism. Teamwork.

Him and Dixie got me in the car and to the emergency ward. I was passing in and out of consciousness, but I did hear the voice of the young emergency ward doctor who had made me identify Knuck's body three days before. He was telling a nurse I must be the father of the most violent family in Little Rock.

Maybe so. But right now, I've got to convince the judge to let me bring Francis home. I might not be doing it the easiest way, and it may take a while, but I'm going to put what's left of my family back together. One fight at a time.

I don't know the law from quantum physics. But I do know right from wrong. Any law that keeps my boy locked up one more minute is wrong. Plain and simple. I know if my boy Francis spends one more day in jail, he's going to die of a broken heart.

I've no doubt that around the world at any given moment, a switch, belt, paddle, razor strap, bamboo stick, seal bone, or fan belt is contacting some little bare bottom somewhere. Nine-tenths of the pain a person suffers over his lifetime is at the hands of his loving parents in the name of discipline. The noise from all the crying kids has been circling the earth without a moments rest for the last ten thousand years.

The most vivid memory I have of my father is not him throwing the ball with me or taking me to the park, but of him standing on the floor furnace grate outside my room unleashing his belt one handed just before he used it on us. To this day, I break out in a cold sweat if I see someone yanking the cord on an outboard motor.

There's a meanness in this world that we can't hardly avoid. It's strung back and forth across our lives like barbed wire. And when we have a chance to clip the barbed wire and we don't, we might as well be stringing it ourselves. I'm going to ask the judge to do something that might not be perfectly legal, but it's better than legal. It's right.

If I have to, I'll get on my knees and beg the judge to let me take my boy home. I accept full responsibility for all the goings on this week. It was all my fault. I should have known better. I've got no business trying to raise a white rat, much less four kids. I know that, now that I've lost fully half of what I started with. More than half if you count pets. And if the deck wasn't stacked against me to start with, I got to try raising a family in a world so ate up with violence it's gnawing its own leg off like a wolf in a trap.

Kill some Canaanites or Hittites or Samsonites and do it in the name of the Lord and they'll write you up in the Good Book and make the little kids memorize your name at Sunday School. Kill a village full of Vietnamese and say it's defending democracy and you're a national hero. Kill an eighteen-year-old boy with a club in Little Rock and say you were defending your castle, and you're a local hero. I guess that will make the person who finally pushes the big red button to start the nuclear holocaust a world hero. Maybe it's time. I don't know. I don't know if I much care anymore. It just don't make sense.

God as my witness, if this judge lets me take him home I *will* have Francis at his arraignment. The Fielder family is through fleeing. How can we leave? I've got a little girl and now a son buried here. If my wife didn't go to mass at the cathedral three times a day, the Pope would pull their franchise. Francis and I have a state championship to win. I have a chance, maybe my last chance, to prove to anybody who still gives a nut that my life hasn't been a total waste. And that neither was my boy's.

I figure I've got one more shot at getting this family thing right. I've got a lot to prove. And a lot to disprove. But mostly, I've got a lot to get my arms around.

❖ ❖ ❖

FIELDER FAMILY FLEES

LITTLE ROCK (UP) -- A manhunt for a former major league baseball player, his youngest son and another minor that involved state and federal law enforcement agencies in five states ended today when Little Rock District Attorney Addison Nickel confirmed that the trio had been located in Canada, staying in a motel under the name A. Einstein and sons.

Jackson "Gooseball" Fielder's youngest son, Francis, who has been charged here with attempted murder in connection with a fight that left one man maimed and another Fielder son dead, was released last week into the custody of his father pending trial. He failed, however, to appear for his arraignment.

D.A. Nickel said that the other minor with the Fielders is the son of the maimed victim and appeared to be staying with Fielder voluntarily. The boy had been wanted as a material witness.

The elder Fielder pitched in 1941 for the St. Louis Brown's but was banned from baseball after World War II because of allegations of treason. The ban was lifted in 1966, too late for Fielder to revive his short career, but in time to remove the stigma from his eldest son who joined the Yankees the next year.

Fielder was the interim head football coach at Nathan Bedford Forrest High School and had led his team to the state playoff finals when the attack occurred November 18. The team, coached by a committee of parents, won the Arkansas State Championship last week.

D.A. Nickel indicated after speaking with Arkansas District Court Judge W. George Gragson, who had released the younger Fielder without bond last week, that he had decided not to seek extradition and would dismiss the charges because of what he termed "extenuating circumstances."

Fielder's wife said in a telephone interview from the family home that she had informed her husband of the plans to dismiss the charges but that he had not indicated any intention to return home. She expressed no immediate plans to join him.

Reached for comment at his home in New York, Fielder's oldest son, Jackson Fielder, II, reliever for the Yankees, stated: "All these years my father's been turning the other cheek. He discovered that the best way to avoid a fight is to declare victory and flee the country. Oh yeah, and take a few prisoners."

THE WISDOM OF SOLOMON

Correct thy son, and he shall give thee rest; yeah, he shall give delight unto thy soul (Proverbs 29:17).

My son, despise not the chastening of the Lord; neither be weary of his correction: For whom the Lord loveth he correcteth; even as a father the son in whom he delighteth (3:11-12).

In the lips of him that hath understanding wisdom is found: but a rod is for the back of him that is void of understanding (10:13).

Chasten they son while there is hope, and let not they soul spare for his crying (19:18).

He that spareth the rod hateth his son: but he that loveth him chasteneth him betimes (13:24).

Foolishness is bound in the heart of a child; but the rod of correction shall drive it far from him (22:15).

The rod and reproof give wisdom: but a child left to himself bringeth his mother to shame (29:15).

The blueness of a wound cleanseth away evil: so do stripes the inward parts of the belly (20:30).

Withhold not correction from the child: for if thou beatest him with the rod, he shall not die. Thou shalt beat him with the rod, and shalt deliver his soul from hell (23:13-14).

... AND OF MOSES:

If a man have a stubborn and rebellious son, which will not obey the voice of his father, or the voice of his mother, and that, when they have chastened him, will not hearken unto them: Then shall his father and his mother lay hold on him, and bring him out unto the elders of the city, and unto the gate of his place; And they shall say unto the elders of the city, This our son is stubborn and rebellious, he will not obey our voice; he is a glutton, and a drunkard. And all the men of his city shall stone him with stones, that he die: so shalt thou put evil away from among you; and all Israel shall hear, and fear. (Deuteronomy 21:18-21).

Rick Norman, former parochial school coach, complains that his knees still ache whenever he passes a football field or a church. He concedes he quit playing baseball because he couldn't hit a curve and quit playing golf because that's all he could hit. Author of *Fielder's Choice* and a 1983 treatise on corporate law, Mr. Norman has always enjoyed storytelling and became a writer and trial lawyer so that he might be paid for exaggerating.

DATE DUE